066120

Bingham, John
Brock and the defector

BROCK
AND THE DEFECTOR

BROCK
AND THE DEFECTOR

JOHN BINGHAM

PUBLISHED FOR THE CRIME CLUB BY
DOUBLEDAY & COMPANY, INC.
GARDEN CITY, NEW YORK
1982

All of the characters in this book
are fictitious, and any resemblance
to actual persons, living or dead,
is purely coincidental.

8 2B 447

Library of Congress Cataloging in Publication Data

Bingham, John, 1908–
Brock and the defector.

I. Title.
PR6053.L283B7   1982   823'.914
ISBN 0-385-18360-7
Library of Congress Catalog Card Number 82–45555

First Edition in the United States of America

BROCK

AND THE DEFECTOR

PROLOGUE

After the rape epidemic and the two murder plots, one of which succeeded brilliantly, life in Melford for Superintendent Brock settled down to the gentle routine he had visualised when he asked to be posted back to his home town after his stint in Northern Ireland. Jane, who never repotted easily, had even grown accustomed to the police house, though she sometimes grumbled about the heating system. So Brock had been satisfied with his life, and even the occasional glimpse he had in the town of his former wife now aroused no emotion. By all accounts she seemed happy with the chartered accountant with whom she had run off when the strain of being a police officer's wife had proved too much, and Brock bore her no ill will any more.

At police headquarters, the Chief Constable interfered little with his work, being content to look decorative on his horse, to be seen at functions wearing his smart uniform, and to spend a day or two a week hunting, shooting, or fishing.

Brock's two favourite sergeants, quick tempered Bob "Ginger" Frost and Glyn "Wally" Jones (with his convoluted Celtic theorising), were working efficiently at the minor crimes in the town. And Assistant Chief Constable Tomkins was peppery as ever. So all was well with the Melford police until Alice and Alexis Schorin, the Russian defector, were foisted on them.

Then all hell had broken loose, one way and another.

But now the trauma was over, and Brock was at last able to get down to the serious business of fishing. The trout fishing had been poor, but during the winter he had had a few successes with pike. The summer months had all been warm and dry and it seemed that they might remain so when he set out with Jane to try his skill and luck on a tributary of the river Mell. The chestnuts were filling out, the sky was blue and the weather prophets had predicted that August would grow even warmer. There was nothing to disturb his peace of mind as he cast his flies along the river skilfully avoiding getting tangled in the willow trees and rushes. In the far distance the cathedral spire reached up to the blue sky. A few yards down the river Jane was sitting with her water colours, making a few quick sketches which she would use for large paintings on some rainy day, or during the winter, though on this particular morning it seemed that another winter could never come.

A water-hen skittered from one bank to another with shrill warning calls. Then all was quiet until a trout took one of his flies and made the sound which gives all fishermen a thrill. The top of Brock's rod bent down and began to shudder as the fish made off towards the clump of rushes into which the water-hen had flown.

He called to Jane that he was into a big one, and asked her to bring the landing net which he had left lying by the side of her folding chair. She put down her sketch book and began to pick her way along the bank with the net.

Meanwhile Brock was in trouble with his fish. After the first indignant rush, the trout felt the restraint as Brock cautiously began to play it. It decided to take the easy way and turned back towards the bank on which Brock stood. He began to reel in his line frantically, taking up the slack as fast as he could. But he could not keep pace with the returning fish.

"I'm going to dam' well lose it, I think," he called to Jane. "He's making for the reeds under the willow here, he'll try and snap the cast."

He had given up trying to reel in the line, and was pulling it in with his left hand, letting it coil on the ground at his feet. For a second or two the line went slack, and he pulled in some more. Then it tightened again and there were more tugs.

"He's still there," he called, as he heard Jane descending the bank to where he stood.

But the line again went loose. "Lost him, dam' it. A big one, too. Probably taken the flies and the cast with him."

Brock rewound the line from the ground at his feet, and then began to reel in the remaining slack. After a short while he said, "I'm caught up in the reeds under the willow!"

He tilted the top of the rod from side to side, pulling gently, thinking that it was just possible that the fish had freed itself and made off leaving the line and cast intact. After a while he laid the rod on the ground.

"I'll have to go in and try and sort it out."

"I'll get my Wellingtons and come and help." Jane began to walk quickly back to where she had been sitting. Brock sighed and carefully descended the bank and bent down and followed the line under the willow to where it led to the reeds. He entered the water carefully, testing the submerged ground for unexpected subsidences, or holes, knowing that more than one angler had got into trouble when his Wellingtons had suddenly filled with water.

He edged forward carefully. The fish had gone. By a freak of fortune, the hook had been freed, but the line remained caught in the reeds. Brock tugged without result. He could see exactly where the line disappeared beneath the willow. A little further on it might still be attached to the cast and flies. He reached up with his left hand and grasped a bough of the willow to steady himself and again cautiously felt his way forward.

Then he stopped, peering at where he could see the end of the cast and where it was still joined to the line. The skin on the back of his neck tingled, and the feeling spread to his whole scalp and was accompanied by a wave of goose flesh on his shoulders and arms. He turned, carefully made his way to the bank, sat down on a jutting outcrop of rock, and put his head in his hands.

He heard the crunch of Jane's feet on the twigs behind him, and her anxious voice.

"You all right, Badge?"

He was known as "Badger" Brock, partly because of his name and partly because his dark brown hair had two or three streaks of white in it.

He got to his feet. "Yes, I'm all right. But don't come any nearer, darling, I beg you. Not a step nearer."

She stopped on the bank above him. A breeze ruffled her heavy blond hair. Her green-grey eyes clouded and the blood did not seem to be reaching her normally pink cheeks. When she spoke her voice was hesitant and shaky.

"Badge! Is there something awful there?"

"Yes, there is."

"Dead?"

"Yes. A man. And very soggy. Stay where you are."

He unwound fishing line from his reel and cut it, snapped off small branches from the willow and cordoned off the area in a wide semi-circle. Then he pointed to a building half a mile away.

"I'm going to phone the office. Tell anybody else who may come along to keep away, or they may have to make statements. That should keep them off. Say I said so. I'll be back when I've phoned."

The larks were still in the blue peaceful sky but in the stream the shadows from the willow made the scene suddenly dark and menacing.

The need to do something practical calmed Brock, and as he made his way to the public house on the hill he told himself that the man did not lie "full fathom five," and the holes where the eyes had been were not pearls, and there had been no "sea change," though admittedly there had been a river change in everything, including the one hand which floated on the water among the reeds, and the cavities where ears had been, and the other hand protruding from the sodden brown sports jacket. For a second he wondered wryly if some fish had had their revenge. He did not know if trout were carnivorous, but pike might have had a passing snack, and perhaps a few other creatures, for in nature nothing was wasted. Wonderful, voracious, merciless, bountiful, patient Mother Nature.

It took some time to walk up the hill to the pub and put through the call to police headquarters, and walk back to where Jane was sitting on the bank waiting for him. He reached her at about the same time as the ambulance and the police with their photographers and notebooks and tape measures. He noted with satisfaction that Sergeant Ginger Frost was with them.

"That body—nobody you know, I hope?" Jane asked.

"Impossible to identify till we have gone through the con-

CHAPTER 1

Alice Robins had blamed the coffee for her wakefulness. She had had four cups because Alexis liked chatting till late, and had talked her into having them. She switched on the bedside light. It was two o'clock. The dawns were arriving early but if she could get to sleep soon, she would have a couple of hours before she would have to leave. Not much, but better than nothing.

Her action awoke Alexis Schorin, and he sat up in bed, instantly alert, and looked at her. She knew what he would say.

"Did I?"

"Did you what, Alexi?"

"Did I talk in my sleep?" he asked in the soft, wheedling almost childlike voice which she found enchanting.

"A little—not much."

"What did I say?"

His voice had changed. The ingratiating tone had gone. He spoke loudly, harshly. He was staring at her, his blue eyes seeming to accuse her of holding something back. She imagined it was the manner he would have used when interrogating a difficult suspect. "Tell me what I said," he shouted. Her heart sank.

All the evening he had been gentle, amusing, courteous. She liked and admired his strength, but she guessed it could be terrible if used without restraint.

She sighed. He was totally unpredictable, but she could tell within a few seconds of meeting him whether it was going to be a good evening or a bad one, and if it were to be a bad evening there was nothing she could do about it. It had to work its own way out of his system. It had been a good evening, but it was a tents of his pockets," Brock replied evasively. "But I think," he began reluctantly and stopped.

He had recognised the dead body and was sad, dark thoughts clouding what had promised to be a day of peace and tranquil pleasure. High hopes and bold plans and optimism—reduced to what? To a sodden lifeless bundle in some rushes under a willow in a slow stream. He began to dismantle his fishing rod, but Jane pressed him.

"Do I know him?"

"Let's go," Brock said, not answering her question. He had no more appetite for the picnic, or indeed for any food anywhere. He saw Sergeant Frost walking over to him and was glad of the prospective release from Jane's questions. In a few seconds he realised he ought to have known better. Impetuous Ginger Frost could always be relied upon to let any available cat out of any handy bag.

"There's a thing!" called Ginger Frost when he was still a few yards away. "It's that journalist, Sam Letts, who was staying at the Blue Boar. They reported he was missing, as you know, but they weren't worried. He hadn't paid his bill, but he had left enough luggage to cover it. He didn't eat much, being a heavy drinker, they never do; actually they seemed quite glad he had gone and they were rid of him."

Brock heard Jane gasp, and put his hand round her shoulder.

"Poor Sam!" she whispered.

"Perhaps he poked his nose into things which didn't concern him," said Frost cheerfully.

"He must have fallen into the river when he'd had too much to drink," Jane murmured.

Frost looked at Brock and winked. "It's the old question, sir—did he fall or was he pushed? I can think of somebody who might have pushed him."

Brock looked at Frost and shook his head. "He was a small timer, a guy who always met the wrong people in the wrong place at the wrong time."

"He certainly met one bloke at the wrong time," said Frost doggedly. But Brock shook his head doubtfully.

bad early morning. She sighed again as she heard the hard, ranting voice:

"Why do I always talk in my sleep when I am with you?"

"Now how could I know?" she pleaded.

"What did you put in my coffee? Tell me that, what did you put in my coffee?"

"Why, nothing, my dear. You poured it out yourself. Both our cups."

"You passed me the sugar! You don't take sugar, do you? There was not much in the bowl. There was more than sugar in the bowl."

"There was only sugar in the bowl, Alexi."

He banged the bed. "What did I say *in my sleep?*"

"Nothing much."

"You keep saying not much, but what, tell me what!"

He put a strong hand on each of her shoulders, gripping them so hard that she winced, and shook her. As tears drenched her eyes, the lenses of her spectacles misted over. Suddenly his tone changed, and he reverted to the coaxing style.

"If it is not much, then it will not take long to tell me, will it?"

She groped under a pillow for her handkerchief.

"You seemed to be dreaming about Odessa, Alexi, darling."

"Odessa?"

She nodded. "You said 'Odessa' two or three times. And 'thieves.' And something about a car market, and the kind, hospitable people. After that you were talking Russian, and I did not understand what you said. You were sleeping restlessly. I expect it was the coffee."

He had lighted a Russian cigarette with its long stiff papier mouthpiece, and was lying on his back, staring at the ceiling, inhaling it greedily, blowing smoke out in big clouds.

"Well, then, it was of no importance. The Odessa people will lean out of their windows as you walk along the pavement, and offer you food or wine, even if they do not know you. Such kind people," he murmured. "And such thieves, the best in all the world, and proud of it. They tell a story that a good

Odessa thief can remove a man's socks without taking off his shoes."

Alexis Ivanovich Schorin laughed, happy with his memories. Alice Robins laughed with him, relieved. She was always uneasy when he was furious and a little afraid, too, and with good reason. More than once, when he had given her a sudden thoughtful look, or asked a question in a seemingly innocent tone, she had wondered if he suspected her. The possibility frightened her, partly because of his physical strength and his unpredictable and potentially violent reactions, and partly for another reason which she had not as yet admitted even to herself.

"If you steal a car in the Soviet Union and can get it to Odessa you are home, safe and dry. It is the best place to sell it. They specialise in re-spraying cars, changing the necessary numbers."

Schorin stubbed out his cigarette and lit another.

"You smoke too much," Alice said mildly.

"Cigarettes can seriously damage your health, HM Government Health warning. Printed on every packet in Britain," he sneered. "It's immoral interference with a citizen's death-wish. In Russia we have more freedom."

"You have?"

"In Russia we also have better education. *And* more freedom. We can smoke ourselves to death if we wish. That is our right, guaranteed by law. Now I tell you another thing—we can go to prison whenever we wish. It is easy and costs nothing. It is the right of every Soviet citizen. In prison food costs nothing. Maybe you might not think it very tasty, with your bourgeois upbringing. So what? If you do not like it you need not eat it. That is your right. You have perfect freedom to starve to death. Nobody will interfere."

Alice smiled. She liked to listen to him when he was in one of his mocking moods. It was better than the wheedling or ranting. She feared the wheedling because it might make her do something she should not do, make some move of which Ducane, sitting snugly in his Intelligence office, might disapprove.

"What are you smiling at?"

"I like to hear you joking."

He tried to look shocked.

"But Alice I am serious! These are important freedoms. Like what happens in Russia if you climb up to the prison roof to protest about something. If you do not get shot when starting the climb you have the freedom to stay there, all night, in the snow, and freeze to death if you wish. Of course if you do not come down next morning in time for work parade, then you will be shot at and probably killed. It will save the government the cost of feeding and housing you."

He walked towards the bathroom. She noted his wide shoulders, narrow waist, muscular legs. A perfect streamlined animal. From the bathroom came the swishing noise of the shower. She felt relaxed and eager to drowse but did not have the chance because, above the sound of the shower, the strident demand of the telephone made her heart begin to pound.

Schorin came out of the bathroom, a bath towel draped round the lower half of his body, his face dripping. She looked at him, a question on her face.

"Are you expecting a phone call?"

He shook his head, dabbing at his face with the towel.

"Shall I answer it? Perhaps it *is* a wrong number," she said.

"Are you mad? It might be the Embassy or the Consulate, they don't get their numbers wrong."

"Could be a misdialling. Anyway, a girl friend is nothing to be ashamed of," she said defensively. "Especially not for a Russian *en poste* abroad."

She could have kicked herself for using the words *en poste*. They were too technical for an alleged simple copy typist earning her living by working for authors.

But Schorin did not seem to have paid any attention. He strode across the room, moved the telephone to the side of the little table, sat down beside it, and lifted the receiver.

"Schorin," he said. A voice quacked.

Alexis Schorin said, *"Da,"* once, and then a second time, then *"niet."* After listening for a few more seconds he continued to speak Russian. Alice did not understand Russian, but there was a tenseness in his voice which conveyed what? Fear?

Anticipation? Excitement at some challenge? She did not know.

She felt a sudden stab of guilt because the bedroom was not bugged. The living room and kitchen and elsewhere, yes. But not the bedroom. She had been adamant about that. Ducane and Sugden had tried to persuade her. "It's a closed shop, all in the family," Ducane had said with his wide froglike smile, and Sugden had said, with his Yorkshire accent: "Aye, lass, remember the Victorian mother's well-known advice to her nervous daughter before marriage. 'Just lie back and think of England, dear.' You might be glad of bugging in the bedroom, if he suspected you and became violent," and Ducane had looked at her with worried hazel eyes but she had still refused.

The feeling of guilt passed in a flash. The bedroom was not bugged but it didn't matter because she guessed the phone would be tapped for incoming and outgoing calls. They could, of course, have bugged the bedroom unknown to her, but she had believed Ducane when he said they wouldn't. Schorin had replaced the telephone receiver, and was slowly dressing.

"Well? Who was it? Wrong number?"

"Just a friend," Schorin said, "Yuri Kuznetsov."

She asked him nothing more, knowing his secretive habits, both natural and professional. She too began to dress, abandoning all hope of further sleep, and heard him softly humming one of his favourite Ukrainian folk songs. Suddenly he stopped singing and faced her.

"Does the name Yuri Kuznetsov mean anything to you?"

"Yuri Kuznetsov? No. Should it?"

"I may have mentioned him."

"If so, I've forgotten. A boyhood friend?"

He had finished dressing and stood looking at her thoughtfully. "A friend from the Intelligence School. Ah, Alice, those were the days! Learning much, yes, but above all getting fit. Jumping into the deep snow from the windows of the little green bungalows each morning! Ski-ing all day. Coming back, drinking great gulps of vodka, a beautiful clean drink—none of your silly little single measures. Eating slabs of bread with pig fat on them, hot from the oven. And now I will tell you a secret!"

Alice watched him, fascinated. "What secret? You never tell me secrets, because you don't trust me, in spite of—what we mean to each other."

His eyes lit up, and he began to comb his bronze-coloured hair.

"Ah, Alice. Listen, it is important! If you cut a hole in a birch tree and hang a cup underneath it overnight, then you will by morning have an ice cold drink which the Greek gods would envy!"

"You are teasing me," pouted Alice. He took no notice. She had finished dressing and moved towards the door.

"I must go now, my love," she said.

He suddenly strode towards her and placed himself between her and the door, blue eyes cold and mocking.

"Back to your masters? Please give Mr. Ducane and Mr. Sugden my kind regards!"

She peered at him, wide eyed, and adjusted her big spectacles.

"What do you mean?"

He held her shoulders and shook her. His voice had reverted to the ranting tone of an interrogator getting impatient. A stab of fear went through her like an electric current.

"Alice, Alice, please. I beg you! Please, this is important!"

She said nothing, largely because she did not know what to say. He shook her again, more violently.

"Alice, listen—tell them that Yuri is in London for the air exhibition."

She still feigned ignorance of what he was talking about. Suddenly he let her go. Once more his voice changed as he adopted the soft pleading tone she found so hard to resist.

"Alice! I want you to know something. Will you listen and not forget?"

"What?"

"Yuri Kuznetsov says I may be recalled to Moscow. I want you to know that if I come over to Mr. Ducane *openly* it is because of you."

He fondled the back of her neck with his right hand, tilted her face up and kissed her gently. Alice prolonged the kiss for several seconds to give her time to think.

She was in a dilemma. She thought that Ducane must want him to stay as a double agent in London as long as possible. She had been the instrument whereby Ducane and Schorin had made contact. From his words it now seemed certain that Alexis Schorin guessed she had been Ducane's secret emissary, encouraging Schorin with remarks about opportunities in the decadent West. And reporting back his reactions. Not that Schorin needed much encouragement. His present words filled her with panic because she did not know what her reactions should be.

She knew she had a certain influence over him. She was by nature gentle, and, with her big grey eyes and large round spectacles, she exuded an air of appealing defencelessness. Ducane had said that her femininity appealed to Alexis because he himself was so strong; it was the old story, the alleged attraction of opposites.

For three years Ducane had been a happy man, and, in a way, she had been a happy woman. Despite his occasional rages and sulkiness, she had enjoyed his company much more than she admitted to Ducane: the discreet dinners, the drives into the country, his gaiety and amusing anecdotes. She knew Ducane must value the information he gave, and she now guessed that Alexis had reached the correct conclusions about the part she had played in the operation. But neither of them spoke about it. She was conscious of a smouldering and increasing resentment against Ducane because he had not told her of his successful approach to Alexis Schorin. It was embarrassing and absurd and she saw no reason for it. But Ducane knew it couldn't last for ever. So did Schorin, and so, in her heart, did she. Alexis Schorin, undercover Russian Intelligence officer, with junior cultural attache cover, was bound to be posted elsewhere in the end. Ducane, Schorin, herself, all three of them must know that good things don't last for ever.

She stroked his cheek, and to gain further time said:

"But your career, Alexi?"

"Career! What are careers?" he protested in his forceful ebullient way. "Careers are nothing, happiness is everything! I am happy here with you."

"Happier than with the KGB?"

"KGB, KGB, all you people talk about is the KGB! I am not a KGB officer, I am a Russian GRU officer. Your clever Ducane will have told you that, didn't he?"

Alice remained silent. Schorin rumbled on.

"Who does the advertising and the publicity for the KGB? How much do they pay the bloddy man? They get value for their money! Not a clever assassination, not a document stolen, not a British traitor caught but it is KGB work! No mention of GRU work, is there? Always KGB, even in Russia."

Schorin shook his head in mock despair. "Yet we are the experts when it comes to military, naval, or air force information. If they want stuff about an RAF engine, or a new naval or military gun, who do they come to? If they want to know the value of documents about these things, who do they ask? Us!"

Schorin stopped, then embarked on a different line. "Brezhnev is a fool, him and all his gang, KGB tools! Russia will be better off without them, that is why I have been helping your Ducane. Oh, Alice, do not try to look surprised and indignant. I know what you are, the GRU knows."

He waved his hand airily, "So you see, if you come with me to Russia, it will be a great GRU triumph, and a slap on the wrist for the KGB."

"It is not on," Alice said dismally. "You may have helped Ducane, and you will still help him when you go to Russia, if you go, and you will be arrested in the end. And shot. And I shall be a widow in Russia. And unable to come home. One of the walking dead. Who's the woman Elli," Alice asked suddenly. "You mentioned her in your sleep. You said Elli ate, and something I couldn't catch."

Schorin laughed. "Not a woman, a man who used to teach me English—Elliet, funny old chap.

"My friend Yuri, who just telephoned, he is GRU, over here for the air show, as I said. He used to be KGB. Still has KGB friends. From the old days. So he warned me. By phone, riskily, because it is so urgent. The GRU know you for what you are. But I think the KGB don't. The KGB is on top now. But it will not always be so. Not when Brezhnev and his gang are gone." Suddenly he began talking fiercely, throwing out short, disconnected sentences.

"Stalin was a great man. A very great man. Stalin loved Russia. All Russians love Russia. I am a good Communist, like Stalin. Brezhnev and his gang must go! His friends the KGB must go! We must start again. In helping Ducane I am helping Russia! There is much work to be done here. I do not know all their agents. And they do not know mine. I have enemies in Moscow, I have enemies here, but I shall win, me and the GRU we shall win."

Alice Robins peered at him through her enormous pale-rimmed glasses, watching him dress hurriedly. Worried and bemused, she was trying, as so often, to sort out the mentality of the man. One part of her mind saw a controlled schizo-phrenic. A man who loved his country but was betraying his country in what he thought was his country's interests. Why? She now guessed he admired Ducane and his organisation. But there was more to it than that. She did not think he admired Britain. He liked the country and often said so in a patronising way. But there was nothing altruistic about this man. She sud-denly realised she loved this dangerous creature, as a keeper will love the unpredictable animals in his charge; and like the keeper she took a fatalistic view about him. Sometimes she thought she could straighten him out, given the right circum-stances. But one day he might turn and rend her. It was an ex-citing risk, a challenge. She drew in her breath sharply. The key lay in the word *challenge*. To Schorin the KGB crowd was a challenge. Pitting his wits against them was a challenge, and the risk added to the excitement. She felt sure that Alexi wished to get rid of the current Soviet government. She was also certain that fundamentally, he preferred Russia to Britain. But not at the moment. At the moment there was clearly a KGB–GRU struggle on, and Alexi was in it, deeply and dan-gerously involved.

She stood uncertainly by the door, Schorin turned away and began to pace round the little bedroom. His next words only increased her dilemma.

"Either I come over completely and openly—or I am posted back to Russia."

She drew in her breath sharply.

"When? Posted when?" she whispered.

"How do I know?" Schorin said impatiently. "Six years, six months, six days even. Yuri doesn't know. He says soon."

"How does he know?" Her voice was hardly above a whisper.

He made another impatient gesture with his hand. "He was in the KGB with me, transferred to the GRU with me, but still sees his old KGB friends in Moscow."

"Where would they post you to, Alexi?"

He clutched his head with both his hands. "How do I know? How the bloddy hell could I? I don't know, Yuri doesn't know, they probably don't know themselves. Maybe Samarkand, maybe the Baltic, maybe Moscow! Buy a bloddy map, take a pin, and shut your eyes and stab, it'll be as good a guess as any."

Alice looked at him. She would have given a month's salary for a few quick words of advice from Ducane. Would Ducane wish to play safe, let Alexi stay *en poste* in London as long as he could, and then call it a day? Or would Ducane welcome his recall to Russia? Had he already made plans how to use him in Russia? Arrangements for briefing and de-briefing, the "live" and "dead" letter boxes, the drops and the pick-ups, the call for an emergency meeting, and the final desperate appeal, "Get me out, I am in mortal danger!" Had Ducane arranged all those things, including the escape route? She felt a wave of panic at the idea of Alexi being caught and shot, and the idea of what they might do to him before he was shot.

She had tried to solve her problem and failed. Better to leave it till she had seen Ducane. Ducane must have foreseen the position, decided on the answer. She looked at her gold wrist-watch. Alexis had given it to her in the early days. He saw her.

"Keep it as a souvenir," he sneered. "The GRU paid for it. Authorised by the Resident."

She felt sickened by the wave of disillusion which swept over her. She took it off and laid it carefully on the bed.

"Keep it for your next bird."

The bitterness in her voice only made him laugh.

"Alice, little Alice! So young, so innocent! They should not let you out without a nurse. Your task for Mr. Ducane was to

—what is the phrase?—soften me up. You succeeded. My task for the GRU was to soften *you* up. I think I have failed. Would you come to Russia with me, if I went back?"

There was no point in beating about the bush now. She could not stop him thinking the truth.

"I would never be accepted in Russia."

"They *would* accept you. You with your knowledge of Ducane and his files would be—most hospitably received by high and low.

"You should know that over here the GRU say I have failed. At least with you, Alice, and they regard you as very important. Come back with me, and they will know I have not failed. I have not failed in other ways, but with you it is—what do you say?—black mark. Come back with me and it will be the Order of Lenin."

"How nice for you," she said.

"We shall be happy. I will finish with it all. You will just answer a few questions now and again. We shall have a flat in Moscow, and a little dacha in the birch woods in the country, and we will cut into the trees and gather the delicious juices as I told you we did. Summer will be long and warm days, and when winter comes we will jump into the snow together, and food will never have tasted so good to you, and the love we will make will never have seemed so good. Alicenka, come with me, and let Mother Russia fold you in her arms as I have done, and always will."

Her disillusion about the wrist-watch had given place to a feeling of shocked surprise, which was replaced in turn by self-reproach. She should have assumed that two could play at the same game. She had tried to lure Alexi; and the GRU or the KGB or both—she was not yet sure—had tried to lure her. It was obvious now.

Alice had opened the door, but now she closed it and walked back into the middle of the room and looked at him with her wary and thoughtful grey eyes.

"How would I get to Moscow?" she asked, to temporise, and saw his blue eyes flash with interest and hope. "Ducane has my passport," she added, all pretence abandoned now.

"Take a day ticket to Boulogne! Then go on to Paris. My

friends will do the rest. Burgess and MacLean managed it. I will meet your 'plane in Moscow. So easy, Alicenka."

"Once you are back, Ducane would blackmail you, Alexi. God knows, he has enough ammunition to use."

"I would report the first sign of it. At once. Capitalist lies and intrigues, I would say. Ducane is a CIA catspaw, I would say, did I not bring Ducane's former secretary with me?"

He was shouting again now.

"You would always be suspect," she murmured. "So would I. They would watch me day and night. Stay here, Alexi. And let us be happy. Then, when the recall comes, and you know it is not just a rumour, make the open jump to Ducane."

It was all out in the open now, every pretence gone.

"I made the jump three years ago, as you know. In secret."

"Half a jump."

"Enough to put me in Ducane's power." He spoke quietly, objectively, without rancour.

"Chicken feed," murmured Alice. "You kept most of the stuff back." His reply surprised her with its frankness:

"I had to, didn't I? A reserve of funds, of a sort, to bribe your bloddy Home Office if I should wish to stay here, if I should decide openly to—*defect*." He spat the word out as if it were bitter aloes. "If I, Alexis Ivanovich Schorin, officer of the GRU, wish to *defect*, I will have to pay my way. Up to now I have told Retchov the Resident what I have given Ducane. I've said I passed it via you, it was my excuse for seeing you, he encouraged me, he believed me."

"You must be mad to think that."

He looked at her and for the first time she noted a look of alarm on his face.

"Why do you say that? Have you any reason to think that?"

"Plenty. And if I came to Russia with you the only dacha they would give us would be in Siberia. And they would consider that giving us the benefit of the doubt. Goodbye Alexi, see you tomorrow?"

"I hope so." He suddenly walked to a small desk, unlocked a drawer and took out a cassette.

"Keep this for me." She took it hesitantly.

"What's on it?"

"Just songs. Ukrainian folk songs. Keep it for me—just in case."

"In case of what?"

He shrugged. "Just—in case."

She put it in her handbag. Her heart was heavy and filled with foreboding. She did not know what she was afraid of, only that a situation which had been filled with fun and spiced with interest, had suddenly darkened.

"Get to know him, get friendly," Ducane had said when he put her into the field. That had been easy. Then Ducane had said, "Keep him happy and contented," and that had been easy, too. She had not only kept him happy but also herself. Now everything seemed to be in a state of flux. And she was tired of the game. She longed for both of them to be rid of the whole thing and free to carve out a new life together. But was it possible, and where? Australia? She sometimes thought there must be as many Iron Curtain defectors in Australia as rabbits before myxomatosis.

She swung round and flung her arms round his neck, and kissed him.

"Take care, my darling," she whispered.

"And you, little Alice," he whispered.

"I think you are in great danger, Alexi. I do not know why. I just feel it. We've done our duty, now let us work for ourselves."

"My work is not yet finished, let me finish it," he pleaded.

"You're hopeless," she said, but she knew in her heart that much of his attraction was his hopelessness, his obstinacy, his courage. At the door she turned and waved briefly.

"See you this evening?" he called.

"I hope so, dear God I hope so."

As she made her way to the outer, front door, she heard the phone ringing again in Schorin's flat, and hesitated, then she went back to Schorin's private door and stood listening. She heard him talking to somebody in Russian.

For a few seconds she stood on the top step outside the front door, looking up and down the street.

CHAPTER 2

Although it was not yet full daylight it was possible to see lamp-posts, parking meters, the numbers on doors. When she left the house in Ebury Street, where Alexi occupied the ground floor and basement, she turned towards Elizabeth Street, again looking up and down the road. At the corner a man in an overcoat was watching his Alsatian dog sniff a lamp-post. Four o'clock in the morning was an unusual hour to take a dog for a walk.

If she continued on her present course, she would pass the man with the dog. She crossed the road, paused, looked ostentatiously at what might have been a wrist-watch, turned, and retraced her footsteps and passed Alexi's house. As she did so a large dark car drew up near the house, hesitated, and moved on slowly. When she passed Number 452, opposite Alexi's place, a light was switched on, curtains were pulled apart for a second or two, and then drawn again.

The car had stopped and the man with the dog was approaching it as if to speak with the driver. She could make out the registration letters, GLR, but not the number. The light still showed from behind the drawn curtains. Was it some bad sleeper or early riser who liked to brew a cup of tea to fill in the time before the day began properly? She could not know and ceased to speculate, since she felt instinctively that she had no time to do so. Logical thought was replaced by emotion, and the emotion was fear.

She was a few yards past Number 452, but she swung round and ran back to the door, her footsteps tapping clearly in the dawn silence. She rang the bell, lengthily and jerkily, to try to signal urgency. The house door was opened, still on the chain, and a querulous voice asked who she was and what she wanted. Through the few inches she saw a lined, whiskery grey face peering at her through steel-rimmed spectacles.

"Let me in, do please let me in!"

She saw the door close hastily. She also saw the car GLR begin to move forward again, and banged on the door with her fist, and called again: "Do please let me in!"

Car GLR was slowing down a few yards away as she heard the old man slowly and reluctantly slide the bolt along the chain and again partly open the door. Behind her, but a yard or two away, she heard a faint crackle as the car went over something in the gutter, and then came the sound of the car door opening.

"I can explain, really I can," she pleaded, and pushed the door open and stepped inside, closing it behind her.

"Now look 'ere miss, you can't just come barging in 'ere like that," grumbled the old man, peering at her more closely. He was dressed in a shabby dressing-gown and pyjamas.

"I'm so sorry, but I think I'm being followed by two men in a car and I'm scared, I hope you wouldn't mind if—"

From a room nearby a woman's voice interrupted: "Oh, let her in, Bert."

"She's in, ain't she, Maudie?"

"Bring her in here, Bert, and give her a cup of tea, poor thing." The old man sniffed and dabbed his nose with a crumpled handkerchief.

"Mrs. Atkins says to go in. Me and the missus, we're taking care of the house while the owners are off gallivanting somewhere. Got to be careful who we let in, right?" He led the way into a front room where an elderly woman sat. She could have been a female replica of Bert Atkins, even down to the whiskers on her chin, and was stirring tea in a pot, peering at it with a suspicious look.

Alice made excuses for troubling her, explaining about the car and the two men. Mrs. Atkins nodded.

"Can't be too careful, dear," she said, and poured some tea into a cup. "Should have let it draw for a few minutes," she muttered. From the hall came the sound of Bert Atkins sliding the chain back on the door. Mrs. Atkins nodded approvingly.

"Nothing like a bolt and chain for keeping folk out. Better than one of these fancy locks, a chain is."

Alice Robins felt a sudden weakness in her legs. She looked pale.

"Sit down for a minute, dear," said Maudie Atkins, staring at her. "Like a nice cup of tea?"

Alice was glad to sit down in an easy chair by the electric fire. But she declined the cup of tea. "It's kind of you, but no, thanks all the same. I expect they'll drive off soon. They kept following me in this big car. Then they had a word with a man."

"Perhaps they was just asking the way, and—"

"Perhaps," Alice agreed. "Perhaps I'm being silly."

"Better safe than sorry, dear."

She poured tea into two cups as Bert Atkins came into the room and sat down next to his wife. They both stared at her over the rims of their tea cups. There was a long silence, broken only by slurping noises as they sipped the hot tea. Alice wished they would say something, but they didn't. She tried to find a topic of conversation, but after a few remarks about the weather she gave up trying.

A French clock on the mantelpiece ticked, the sound being the only noise to break the silence. Maudie and Bert Atkins continued to stare at her, eyes unblinking behind steel spectacles. Alice found their staring disquieting, though she did not know why. Now the suspicious look had disappeared and been replaced by something more difficult to describe. It seemed to be a mixture of interest and wariness.

Conscious of her very ordinary appearance, she did not like being stared at, and she found the intensity of the interest unnerving. The old man fetched a pipe from another table.

"Well, I'll be getting along," she said brightly. "I'm most grateful to you for—"

"I'll just finish me tea in peace, then I'll maybe let you out," Bert Atkins said.

Alice felt a constriction of the muscles in her throat.

"Maybe?"

"Bert means he'll have a look round first, to see if the coast's clear, miss." The old woman continued to look at Alice with her concentrated stare. "I don't think I know your name, miss."

"Robins, Alice Robins."

Maudie Atkins took a sip of tea. "I think I've seen you before, miss. I often sit in the window watching people come and go. Helps to pass the time. Do you often come to these parts, miss?"

"I have a friend who lives opposite."

Mrs. Atkins adjusted the spectacles on her nose. "Ah, yes, that's it, dear. What they call a boyfriend, these days." Mrs. Atkins made a noise which sounded like a soft discreet cackle.

"I really must be off." Alice again got to her feet.

"No hurry, dear," Mrs. Atkins said.

"Still quite early," Bert Atkins agreed. They both looked at her woodenly.

"It's a Mr. Shorben," Bert Atkins said.

Alice corrected him. "Schorin, not Shorben."

"Lives in the lower part of the house, top half's empty," Mrs. Atkins said. "They'll have squatters there if they are not careful, mark my words. Nice young man, your Mr. Schorin. I take his laundry in for him sometimes if he's not there. Russian, I believe. From the Embassy or something."

"I'll let myself out," Alice said abruptly.

"Not without a key, you won't," the old man gave a wheezy laugh. "Door's locked, ennit? She come in without asking, not so much as a by-your-leave, but she can't go without asking, can she? And I haven't finished my tea, have I?" He looked at his wife uncertainly, as if waiting for some sort of instruction. Then he poured the remainder of his hot tea into the saucer and sucked it down noisily. When he had finished Mrs. Atkins nodded.

The old man got up and shuffled to the door. Alice heard him unlock the door and slide the chain back. At first, glad to escape from the menace in the street, she had found the place warm and comforting, but now she found the old couple vaguely menacing.

She made a firm effort to pull herself together. There was

not the smallest indication that they were not what they purported to be. They were right to be cautious about letting her in. Mr. Atkins was right to keep her in the house till he was sure the coast was clear. And if their stare showed unusual interest, that was natural: they had seen her go in and out of Alexi's and drawn their own conclusions. Perhaps they were wondering what he saw in her. So what? She often wondered herself. Yet the uneasiness remained and disturbed her. From the noises outside she judged the street door to be open. She had barged her way in, and now she could barge her way out.

She got up quickly and moved to the half open drawing-room door and had put her hand on the door knob when she heard a slight movement behind her, and felt her forearm grasped in a surprisingly strong grip, and looking down saw the veined hand of Mrs. Atkins, and noted how the grip tightened.

"Wait till Mr. Atkins reports back, miss." Alice Robins felt her throat constrict again. The words "report back" came oddly from an old woman like Mrs. Atkins. She could imagine a KGB operator using the words in the same peremptory way.

From the front door Bert Atkins's voice drifted back: "They must have turned again, miss, they were talking again to that man you saw. Then they moved off. Gone now, car, man, bloomin' dog, all gone."

She took a deep breath, snatched her arm free, and ran out of the room, making for the open front door. Bert Atkins was standing with his back to her. At the sound of her footsteps he turned round, and she saw the small automatic in his right hand. She stopped at once. Barging past an old man who was probably going to let you in anyway was different from pushing past a man with a gun, however old and frail. Bert Atkins coughed wheezily once more.

"They've gone," he said again.

"I suppose they have," Alice murmured wearily. "Now what? And why the gun? I'm not as fierce as all that."

"Can't be too careful, like my missus said. We live in stirring times. More's the pity."

She looked briefly over her shoulder when the woman who called herself Maude Atkins also coughed softly, and said:

"Let her past, Bert. We can't hold her against her will, not indefinitely, if she wants to risk it. Give our regards to Mr. Ducane, miss."

"And to Mr. Sugden," muttered Bert Atkins. He had put his automatic back into his dressing-gown pocket and had stepped aside to let her pass. "Sure you won't have a nice cup of tea, miss?"

"Oh, no! No, thank you all the same."

They were still staring at her in the intense way she had noted before. Then they looked at each other. The woman shrugged very slightly. Alice had not acknowledged their greetings to Ducane and Sugden. As she shakily made her way down the front steps to the pavement, she glanced back at them. They were looking questioningly at each other.

It was as though they were wondering if they had done the right thing in letting her go. She hurried along the road, in case they changed their minds.

As she neared the end of Ebury Street she heard what sounded like a car backfiring twice, and stopped and looked back. But the light was still burning in Schorin's room, and there was nobody in the street. She sighed with relief. There was no back door to his house. So he was all right. And she was all right. At least for the moment.

She had to walk as far as Sloane Square before she found a taxi. She heard the distinctive sound of a diesel-fueled cab behind her, and saw it crawling hopefully after her with the "For Hire" light on. She signalled to him, he stopped a few yards in front of her.

Alice Robins walked up to the cab, her lips set in a firm line, and gave her address in Hornton Street, Kensington, and got into the cab. Fifteen minutes later she was home, had undressed for a quick shower, and filled a kettle of water to heat for the cup of tea she had not drunk in Ebury Street. While she ate a slice of rye bread and some cheese, she noted in her diary the cost of the taxi fare to add to her expenses claim which, among other things, she would give Ducane shortly.

She did not eat much. She had a pain in the region of her

heart. But there was nothing organically wrong with her heart. She knew that, because she had had similar pains six years before, when she was twenty-four, and Pat had left her after two years of happy marriage. Happy for her, but apparently not happy enough for him. He had run off with a girl from the office Registry, and settled in Jamaica, where incidentally, he could not be reached for alimony. He had paid it for a while, and then he had stopped, and according to her lawyer there was nothing she could do about it. Not that she wished to. The less the connection with him the better. She was determined to make herself independent.

But she had seen the office doctor when the pain persisted, and queued up with others, most of whom were waiting for an anti-influenza injection. Old Dr. Tiller had listened to her heart, and shaken his grey head. He knew about her situation. Everybody in the office did. Naturally. But he asked a few questions.

"How did you part? On friendly terms? Not that I believe in the myth of friendly divorces."

"I did not hate him," she had answered carefully. "The day he cleared out was pretty awful. I remember I had hard-boiled a dozen eggs and hid them among his clothes in his luggage. He was so disorganised about food. Then I walked to Palmer's Green and sat on a bench in the sun and blubbed a bit."

"It probably did you good."

She shook her head. "It didn't do me any good at all. I felt lousy." Dr. Tiller looked up from the prescription he was writing.

"There's nothing wrong with your heart. People think heartache doesn't exist, that it's made up by romantic fiction writers, but it does. It'll pass. One day you'll wake up and find the sky is blue after all, and there's a funny noise in the trees and it's those dam' birds singing and keeping people awake. I've given you a prescription for drinamyl, fifty, with five repeats at intervals of not less than two months, which means a slight gap, but that'll do no harm. They calm you down if you're over excited, and pick you up if you are depressed. Take two a day, one in the morning and one in the afternoon, but not after four o'clock. They should help. I believe they are going to ban them, on the grounds that they are addictive and are abused. So's gin. And whisky. And coffee. Sometimes I despair of higher authority. It always thinks it knows best. And don't drink too much alcohol, too much doesn't help depression. Alcohol only increases the mood you happen to be in. Now, if you'll excuse me, I have to fix up one of your colleagues with splints so that he has an excuse for not going somewhere he doesn't want to go. It was either that or a collar for a broken neck, and he preferred the leg splints."

He had patted her on the arm as she went out of the room. "Cheer up, Alice. You'll be all right in the end." So she had been, she thought, as she chewed the rye bread and slices of Dutch cheese, but not only because of the drinamyl.

Alexi had brought her to life again. Sometimes tender, sometimes rough. Sometimes enchanting, sometimes bullying. Never dull. "Keep him happy," as Ducane had said. In the end it was a two-way switch. Alexi had made her happy, too. Thoughts of him even when he was not with her, occupied her mind. Alexi was the lifeboat into which she had scrambled from the wreckage of her married life.

The frail cocoon around her happiness was in danger of being shattered. She got up to take her breakfast things to the sink to wash them up, and caught sight of herself in a wall mirror, and paused to assess what she saw.

"I'm a small, dull mouse," she thought. And if Alexi went, to Russia or Eternity or both, what would be left?

Her upper lip trembled as it always did when she fought to keep back tears. She thought she might doze for an hour or two before she left to see Ducane at eleven-thirty. She was finishing the washing up when she heard the telephone ringing in the living-room, and dried her hands quickly.

"Duty officer here," a voice said. "Could you come and see Froggie Ducane at ten o'clock instead of eleven-thirty? Something has happened."

"Yes, I can. What has happened?"

"I can't tell you on the phone."

"Something nasty, something bad?"

"I don't know if it's bad, depends how you look on it," said the duty officer cheerfully, and laughed.

"I'll be along," Alice Robins said, and felt her upper lip quivering again as she remembered the two bangs she had heard in Ebury Street and had thought was a car backfiring.

CHAPTER 3

Ducane's real surname, as registered on his birth certificate, was Vandoran, but there had been inconveniences, such as a tendency for people to spell it Van Doran, or even Van D'Oran. It was especially troublesome when trying to book a table in a restaurant by phone. For many years, when active exclusively in the field, he had called himself Ducane, and the name had stuck when he was promoted to a more sedentary post. In the end, since everybody obstinately called him Ducane, he had given up the struggle, and he now even appeared in the office staff directory as Ducane. Regarded as an operation, it was the only one in which he acknowledged complete failure. He had been beaten by his own colleagues.

Her agitation made Alice Robins arrive at about nine o'clock instead of ten, and he was sitting at his desk gently massaging his forehead. It was the third day of the migraine, and the piercing pain had gone. Only a soreness remained. That was how his migraines went nowadays. The early attacks, a few years ago, had been accompanied by the classic half-vision; and the first attack, when he had been able to see only half his face in a looking glass had been not only agonisingly painful but alarming. Now, every month or two, the attacks brought only the pain. Pain-killing tablets made little difference the first day or two. He thought that people who airily advised him to "take a couple of aspirins" had never experienced a migraine. But by the third day pain-killers helped and he chewed a couple now. He had taken a couple at six o'clock with an early morning cup of tea, and the present two would have to last till noon. He could take two more in the afternoon, and so the day would drag on. By tomorrow it should be mostly gone, and he would be free of it for a month or two unless some undue stress brought it back.

As he swallowed the last grains of the tablets he gazed out at
Regent's Park below. Through the lingering mist he could just
see part of the Snowdon Aviary. He heard the croaking bark
of an impatient seal. Bark as it might, it would have to wait a
few hours before a keeper threw fish.

The door opened quietly, just wide enough to allow his secretary, Doreen, to put her head round it.

"Alice is here down below! She's not due till later. My *dear*,
isn't it too, *too* tiresome of her! And you with your poor head,
darling!"

"I'll see her now," he snapped. "I sent for her."

Doreen went out. She called everybody darling. At first her
affected accent had irritated him, and in retrospect he wondered how she had put up with the off-hand way he treated
her. But, as the months passed, her total devotion combined
with her faultless efficiency had won him over. That and the
fact that when it came to scandal and gossip she never missed
a trick. He sometimes thought that she must read every para-
graph of every national newspaper, and remember the contents. There was hardly a prominent name mentioned about
whom she had not got something filed away in her orderly
mind. And she either knew them or knew somebody else who
knew them. Moreover she had a rough side which amused him.
If occasion demanded it she could swear like a trooper. Once,
he had seen her eyes, normally like brown, licked toffee-ap-
ples, flash with hot anger. "You bum!" she had said to one of
his colleagues, "You absolute *bum!*"

Ducane was always known as "Froggie" because in some
ways he resembled one. He carried no superfluous fat, and
though often immobile for long periods, hands flat on his desk,
palms downwards, fingers pointing inwards, hazel eyes watchful in a sallow face, he could spring very quickly if he was interested enough to do so, which wasn't often. All this was in itself enough to explain his nickname. His mouth perfected the
picture: thin, with a short upper lip, it stretched widely across
his face giving the impression that he was always half smiling.

For some years he had courted a secretary in the Service
called Freda, who had eventually turned him down. Inevitably
Doreen knew about it.

"*My dear,*" she had said, carefully painting her finger-nails.

"When I asked him how Freda was, and he told me what had happened, I *swear* he was smiling."

"Can't blame Freda," the section Registrar had said. "Who wants to be married to a cold frog?" Doreen's eyes flashed.

"But *darling,* who but a frog would want to be married to cold Freda?" Doreen had no amorous feelings for Froggie Ducane, and was inclined to agree with the Registrar, but nobody was allowed to attack her frog, unless they wished to be lacerated by her well manicured nails or attacked by a sharp tongue.

Now she bustled into Ducane's room again holding some papers. "Alice is on her way up. And those *ghastly* transcription people have produced a shower—but a *shower* of tripe for you," she said indignantly as she placed typewritten pages on his desk. Ducane looked at the pages, and remained staring at them so long she thought he had fallen asleep.

"Dar-ling!" she said testily. "Have you fallen asleep? I *do* sometimes think you suffer from *narcolepsy.*"

He raised his eyes.

"Nark what?"

"Narcolepsy, Froggie dear—dropping off to sleep at the most *impossible* times. Poor Alice is wilting, but *wilting* while *you* nod off."

"Show her up," Ducane said abruptly, and from the tone of his voice Doreen knew it was not a moment for further facetious remarks. "And tell Beryl I want the gist of any further phone calls last night immediately. But *immediately,* understand? And the full text as soon as possible. Right?"

Doreen nodded silently and went out of the room closing the door softly behind her. Ducane gently stroked a small vein in his forehead which had swelled up with the migraine. He read the phone-call transcript again. He read the top copy a third time. It was the gist of a phone conversation:

03.17 hours. From notes only. Incoming call for Schorin. Male caller.

Schorin seems to be friendly. They exchange pleasantries in English. Schorin sounds surprised and pleased to hear caller's voice. Schorin seems to be an intimate friend. Caller says he is in London for the airshow. Schorin says he would like to go, too, and take a girl friend. (Caller laughs). Could caller get tickets? Caller says he will try the Embassy, but sounds doubtful. Tickets in much demand for air attaché and friends. Couldn't Schorin try the Embassy? Schorin says he could but— Schorin stops, then adds, "You know?" Caller says yes, he understands. (Caller is speaking from call-box in Marloes Road, Kensington. Pause, while caller inserts coins in phone box.) Caller still speaking English. Says he has been talking to old friends in Leningrad. He stressed words "old friends," adds "you know?" Schorin says he thinks he does. Had a good evening drinking, talking of old times at the—. Schorin interrupts quickly, saying "yes, yes." He asks caller to continue, but to speak in Russian. From now on they talk in Russian. Condensed translation:

Schorin says he has his English girl friend with him. Caller laughs. Caller says Schorin is to be recalled to Russia. Maybe soon maybe not for some time, he doesn't know. During ensuing conversation Schorin at first sounds interested, but his voice slowly changes and he seems dismayed. Asks, why the recall? Promotion? A desk job in Moscow? Caller laughs, says no. Far from it.

Schorin interrupts again. (Still in Russian) Sounds agitated. He tells caller his girl will be leaving in about twenty minutes. Will caller ring back in thirty minutes? He does not think his girl friend speaks Russian. But one can never be sure, can one? Not that it matters, in one way, because he assumes his phone is tapped by the British, but it does matter in another way: he has unfinished business with his girl friend. Caller laughs, asks "How much unfinished?" Schorin does not laugh, says, "Not that, but it is important." Caller promises to ring back. Call ends 03.21 hours.

Outside in his secretary's room Doreen's voice rose above the clatter of the typewriter of the girl who shared the room with her.

"Alice, darling, how wonderful to see you. Froggie will be *delighted*. Poor Froggie, he's had another of his *awful* migraines. No, of *course* you must go in." Her voice died away. Alice opened Ducane's door and went in and paused uncertainly.

Ducane's face lit up. He got up to greet her.

Ducane always said that the greatest sacrifice he had made in his professional life was when he gave up having Alice as secretary and put her into the field. He felt as badly about it as when his wife, Isabel, had left him for a Civil Servant in the Ministry of Agriculture and Fishery. In fact, on balance, rather worse. Isabel had never been happy as the wife of an Intelligence Officer, and never would have been. She was unhappy when he worked late at night in the office or went abroad. And that made him unhappy too, which distracted his mind.

Alice sat down in the arm-chair by Ducane's desk and stared at him, grey eyes wary, observant, and thoughtful.

"What's happened?" she asked. Her mouth was dry.

"That's happened." He handed her the transcript. "It alters things a bit, doesn't it?"

She read it. "He told me a good deal. Is he all right? Night duty dog told me something nasty had happened."

Ducane looked closely at her pale face. "As far as I know he's all right. But Doreen says Transcript have just telephoned. There's more stuff on the way. They didn't say what. But they sounded excited. The stuff came over a few hours ago, but the day people have only just got around to it. Lazy slobs." He was still looking at her intently, eyes thoughtful. To break the silence she licked her lips and spoke, abruptly, the words coming out in a sudden gush.

"I'm blown as an agent. I blew my cover, and Schorin blew his, too. There was no avoiding it.

"He guessed I set him up for you," she added. Ducane nodded, unperturbed.

The news that, according to Ducane, Alexi was still alive, sent a wave of relief through her. But it was instantly followed by a resurgence of resentment against Ducane.

"You let me down. Why didn't you tell me you had approached Alexi a long time ago, and that he was working for you? He said he might have to go back to Russia, and would I go with him? If not, he might go alone. I didn't know what the hell to do," continued Alice, pent up anger in her voice. "I didn't know whether to encourage him to go or encourage him to stay in London as long as possible and then defect openly. And why didn't you tell me about Bert and Maudie Atkins? They scared the life out of me. Whenever I asked about Alexi and the possible approach, a few times, you replied vaguely that you thought you were making progress, that's all you said. It wasn't fair."

"I don't deal in fairness. I fight to win. You should know that. I wanted you to go on reporting every detail as before, to see how he was reacting to his new position with me. I calculated that if you knew that the operation had succeeded you might grow lax."

"Have I ever been lax?"

"Well, no, but—anyway, he's holding something back. You know that."

She nodded reluctantly. "Something about a chief nestling."

"I think you are getting keen on him. Are you?"

"I find him—usually—quite attractive," she admitted coolly.

"Yes. Well. Time to call it a day."

She changed the subject. "He had that call last night from a pal who was with him in the KGB. Alexis may be recalled to Moscow or somewhere. It's not known when."

"I know." He pointed at the telephone transcript on his desk.

"I thought you might. When and if he goes he wants me to go with him. He asked me last night, as you know."

Ducane wasn't falling for that one. "I only know what you've told me. The bedroom isn't bugged, I promised it wouldn't be. What did you reply?"

"I said I wouldn't, I said I'd never be accepted over there. I said if he went back you'd get at him, force him to work for you—over there."

Ducane smiled. "So I would."

"I told him to stay in London as long as he could, then come over to you permanently. Openly."

"Defect?"

"Yes. I just didn't know in which direction to steer him."

Ducane had left his desk and was striding round the room when Doreen came quietly in and laid a sheet of paper on his desk. After a few seconds he stopped and stared out of the window at the Zoo.

"The mist's lifted," he murmured, then swung round and said: "He'll stay, he'll obey me. He must. He knows it. In case he's forgotten I'll remind him. If he doesn't, I'll blow him to the Soviet Embassy. Discreetly, of course, just enough to let them come to their own conclusions, and I'll fix it with the Home Office so that there will be no asylum for him here, and with the Foreign Office so that there will be no asylum for him anywhere else."

"He's valuable, and you'd lose him." Desperation was in her voice.

"Yes, I would. It would be a warning to the rest, to do what they're told. He'd be a dead man." An idea seemed to occur to him. He paused by her chair, and put a hand lightly on her shoulder.

"Come to think of it, I don't need to tell him, you can tell him all that, since you are so close to him, dear."

She brushed his hand off her shoulder and stood up. "You couldn't do that!"

"Try me and see."

"You couldn't live with yourself afterwards!"

"I would make a good attempt," Ducane muttered. "I would get over his assassination in about thirty seconds."

Panic at the idea of breaking her association with Alexi, and a return to her former life in a bed-sitter swept over her and mingled with her shock at Ducane's ruthlessness.

"I think you stink," whispered Alice. "I think you absolutely stink!"

"I suppose I do. Sometimes. It's what I'm for."

Yet Ducane knew she was right, he couldn't do it. But he wasn't going to let her know it. He was fond of Alice but if he had to lose her friendship it couldn't be helped. From the Zoo came the sound of lions roaring for the meat they would not

get that day, because it was Wednesday. Or would they? Food
used to be withheld once a week in the interest of their health,
because they were cooped up in cages. He wondered if food
was still withheld on Wednesdays, since most of them now had
more room for exercise. He pressed his forehead. The pain had
returned and he knew it was caused by stress and anxiety
about what he must do. A target in love with an agent was
okay, but an agent in love with a target was bad news. He
hated man-woman situations. They always ended in tears,
drama and scenes. And in headaches. He braced himself
against the storm he knew must come. So far there had only
been a freshening of the breeze.

"You've done well, Alice dear," he said again. "Now I think
the time has come for you to pack it in. In your own interests
as well as mine."

"You can't really mean it. He needs my support." But in her
heart she knew he did mean it, though she still found it hard to
believe. A cold hand seemed to be pressed on her heart, making her shiver at the prospect of the grey dreary years ahead.
Ducane sat down and swivelled his chair so that he could look
her full in the face.

"It's time for you to come back into the office, be my secretary again. Doreen will make a fuss but that can't be helped."

"Break it off forever?"

"The job's over, Alice. Engineer a few rows, taper it off
slowly, or have a big row, and have a clean break. It won't be
difficult. You've always jumped well, landed on all four paws
like a good cat."

"Three perhaps, I'm not sure about four."

"That's because you're in love with him."

She made no comment, looking at him helplessly.

"Aren't you?" he persisted. "You're in love with a Russian
spy, one of my agents has fallen in love with a target, now I've
experienced everything," he said bitterly. "I blame myself, I
should have known better."

He gazed into her grey eyes, expecting to see indignation,
but he only saw mistiness and a quivering upper lip. He gritted
his teeth and ploughed on relentlessly: "You'll have to drop

him. Do it any way you like. Just do it, that's all. Engineer a
quarrel, walk out."

She swallowed and said softly, "I don't know that I want
to."

"Probably not, but you'll have to. It's an order. You've become a security risk. I can't afford that in this case."

Alice Robins could change her mood almost as quickly as
Alexis Schorin could change his.

"And if I refuse?" Her voice was suddenly tinny. Ducane
was relieved because he could cope with stubborn opposition
easier than with tears, which always threw him off balance.

"If you won't break with him, he will have to break with
you, Alice."

"And if he won't?" Alice Robins gulped. "He said that if he
stayed in England and went on helping you as long as he
could, it would be—because of me." Ducane laughed, but it
was a humourless sound.

"The Russians are strange, emotional people, capable of inventing more lies in sixty seconds than any other people, and
believing the lies themselves. If they lie for fun it's called
vranyo. If it's with malice aforethought it's called *lozh*. There
are also, of course, just straight lies, produced instinctively, as
a matter of habit. He'll break with you if I tell him to."

She did not press him. After the alarms of the night, she had
come to him, with fear in her heart; then had come the joyful
news that Alexi was all right. Now, instead of sympathy, came
Ducane's announcement that her small shell of warmth and
happiness was to be broken. The anger and resentment she had
felt because Ducane had not confided in her about his successful approach to Alexi was forgotten: a minor irritation compared with the cloud of dismay and depression which now
enveloped her. Outside the hot July sun beat down on the Zoo.
But in Ducane's room it was suddenly November.

Ducane rose, walked around a while, then plumped himself
down in his chair and again picked up the typewritten sheet
Doreen had just put on his desk.

"All right," she said, "I'll have a clean break." Ducane took
no notice. He was frowning, reading more attentively the piece

of paper in his hand. "I'll have a clean break," Alice Robins said more loudly, and burst into tears. "A clean break with *you!*"

She got up and moved towards the door.

Ducane looked up from the piece of paper Doreen had brought in. "You're joking, sit down, you're overtired. I'll get Doreen to bring us in some coffee."

She didn't sit down. "I'm serious. I've done enough for Queen and Country. I'm going to look after myself now. Sorry. It's been fun. In a way."

She turned again to the door.

"Just a moment," Ducane said. "Look at this." She turned back and took the piece of paper and read:

Immediate. From notes only. Translated from Russian. 05.57 hours. Incoming call for Schorin. Voice sounded identical with previous caller. Caller now identified as Yuri Kuznetsov. He apologises for being late, but wished to be —(he hesitates)—*be careful*. Schorin understands. Caller refers to earlier mention of meeting "old friends." Schorin says, "yes, yes," impatiently. Yuri refers to brawl in Soho pub recently. Moscow was displeased because Schorin lost his head and claimed diplomatic immunity drawing attention to himself. Should have given a false name and paid the fine. Or gone to prison if necessary. Schorin says thanks very much. Yuri laughs, but says Moscow recalled incident in Odessa some years ago when Schorin told a discontented Russian air force pilot that he might point his 'plane towards the West next time he flew. He might find things better there. Especially—Yuri laughs—if he brought a valuable aircraft with him fitted with new devices. Schorin is furious, says it was only a joke, "they" had believed him. Schorin says he knew pilot was a KGB informant. Yuri sounds doubtful. How did Schorin know? Schorin says angrily, "because he was *also* one of *my* informants, that's why. He was always grumbling, he said I did not pay him enough." After a long silence, Yuri says Moscow claims Schorin's English girl friend is a British

agent, that she has "set him up" somehow. Schorin starts
to shout. "She is, I know that. I told Moscow. It is an operation, Moscow agreed to it." Talk again becomes garbled. But Yuri is heard to say, "The Resident is ordered
to send you back tomorrow evening." Schorin is shocked
and astounded. "Why so sudden? What about my nestlings. Those I have taken years to hatch and rear?" Yuri
is heard to say that no doubt they would be contacted by
somebody else. Schorin's bewilderment changes to rage
and suspicion. Conversation garbled, each talking over the
other's voice. During a lull Schorin is heard to say: "Yuri,
are you a true friend, or have you been told to—" Schorin
does not finish his sentence. Conversation broken by
sound of what sounded like car back-firing. Small thud
which might have been Yuri's phone receiver knocking
against side of phone box. Schorin shouts his name two or
three times. Gets no reply. Starts to shout again. Mentions
KGB bastards. "I'll fix them, if it's the last thing I do, I'll
get them, I'll get them." Rants on about KGB treachery,
gets no response. Replaces phone.

Alice handed the piece of paper back to Ducane.

"What's it mean?"

"It means somebody is dead and Alexis Schorin is very
angry. It means Kuznetsov, a GRU agent, has been killed
while warning his friend Alexis Schorin." Ducane gazed
dreamily across the Zoo, where the lions, giving up hope, had
ceased complaining.

Ducane opened a desk drawer and took out a piece of paper.

"Loose Minute from the All Highest on the fourth floor," he
said. "I'll read it to you. 'Officers will advise all their agents to
take exceptional precautions for personal safety. According to
Top Secret sources an inter-departmental struggle, which in-
cludes the use of violence, has broken out between the KGB
and the GRU. Four British subjects in the Midlands and West
Midlands, have died in unusual circumstances in the last five
weeks—J. Smith, K. Bailey, R. Barnes, and L. Parker. Two
died in curious road accidents, and two from alleged sudden
heart failure. All had files in this office. Two were known to us
as KGB men, and two as GRU men. Thus the score is even.'"

Ducane put the Loose Minute back into his drawer.

"The score was even until last night," he said briefly. "There is another difference. The latest victim was a Russian, a GRU man."

Ducane smiled delightedly, rubbing his hands with pleasure.

"Splendid, isn't it!"

"If you think a man's violent death is good news, yes. Splendid, I suppose." Her voice was sullen.

"Don't you see! It's hotting up, fratricidal strife, civil war, they're killing each other now! They'll be tearing each other apart, doing our work for us! I see all sorts of amusing developments and possibilities!"

But all Alice saw was Alexis in danger. Doreen came in with another page from the transcribers.

"More stuff, darling! Won't they ever stop?" Ducane snatched the report from her, read it, and handed it to Alice.

06.15 hours. Schorin is in living-room. Shouting into our microphone, apparently using it to get message through: Message for Ducane or Sugden. I am making the jump to you. Hope to be in safe house at eleven-thirty hours.

Ducane pressed the bell-button on his desk. Doreen came in.

"Tell Reg Sugden to see me. At once. Tell him Operation Skip is on. And tell him to bring a razor and toothbrush."

He winked at Alice.

"You'd better go with Schorin. To comfort him. He'll need it now, by God he'll need it!"

Alice left the room. Her thoughts and emotions were muddled; joy and relief that she could still be with Alexi, at least for a while, were mixed with renewed fears for his safety, and for her own tenuous hold on modest happiness. On her way back to her flat to pack a few things, she thought with a trace of bitterness that renewed fears would not worry Alexi. If anything he would find it exhilarating.

When Alice had gone, Reg Sugden came in. Ducane said: "Schorin is making the jump. He'll be at the safe house. You'd better go down to Melford with him. Alice'll go with you. But she's blown her cover."

"Aye, well it was bound to happen sometime. The lass couldn't go on indefinitely." Sugden's deliberate way of speaking and his Yorkshire accent sometimes irritated Ducane.

"She didn't need to fall in love with him," snapped Ducane. "She wanted to pack up working for us till she heard that Schorin was defecting. Why had she got to fall in love with him?"

"Sometimes you can't help it. Any more than you can help falling out of love," added Sugden, putting a match to his pipe.

Ducane swivelled round in his chair and gazed out towards the Zoo, guessing that Sugden was thinking of Rachel Levin, whom Sugden had ditched and who had taken an overdose of sleeping tablets and a great deal of whisky. It was years ago. But the burden of guilt still lurked round Sugden. Nowadays he was usually free of it. Yet it was always there, off stage but crouching in the wings, ready to spring.

"Of course it could be a plant, Reg. Schorin and the others must have known the bedroom was not bugged but that the telephone was tapped. They could have used the phone to set things moving. Couldn't they?"

"You so bloody sharp you'll cut yourself one day." Ducane ignored him. "After all what's he given us so far, Reg? Chicken feed."

"Keeping stuff back for just such a situation as the present one? Bargaining material?"

It was one of Sugden's functions, mutually acknowledged, that he should be an agent provocateur for Ducane, always taking an opposite point of view, drawing Ducane out, forcing him to test his theories, making him hesitate before taking action. A dour unpopular rôle for which his obstinate north-country temperament suited him ideally.

Sugden put another match to his short, stubby pipe. "What about the man killed in the phone box, Yuri Kuznetsov, who warned Schorin? That's what sparked Schorin off."

"Maybe that is what we are supposed to think. Perhaps that's why Yuri spoke so freely on an open telephone line. Is that in keeping with KGB or GRU methods—unless they wanted us to hear it?"

Sugden said nothing for a few moments. The logical corollary was so unpleasant and far fetched that he was reluctant to put it into words. But he finally said:

"If Schorin's a plant, a fake defector, then Schorin, according to your theory, must have known about the Yuri assassination plan."

"That's right."

"But Yuri Kuznetsov was Schorin's old friend. We know that from the files."

"That's right," Ducane said again in a wooden voice. "It didn't help him, did it? Well, you'd better get going, I suppose. Don't tell Alice."

"Don't tell her what?" Sugden asked.

"What I said—about Schorin possibly being a plant."

"Perhaps he isn't."

Sugden left the room. "Why do I do this work?" Ducane asked his secretary when she brought in his mid-morning coffee. "Surely there are easier ways of earning money?"

Doreen laughed. "Darling Froggie, it's a question of *Job Satisfaction*, surely you know *that?*"

"All I know is, I'd like to wake up in the morning and think, what the hell am I going to do today? I'm fed up with responsibility for other people's lives."

She took his empty coffee cup and went out, and in the outer office met Reg Sugden, who had come back to clarify a few points with Ducane. He drew back to let her pass.

"Froggie mucked up that one. Nearly lost Alice," he said grimly. "It's not so much what you do but when and how you do it that matters. He should have known that Schorin, in Alice's view, is her last chance of romance. She wants to hang on to it and she'll fight like hell to keep it. Her life is going to sleep, getting up, eating a bit and drinking a bit, and seeing Schorin. And Froggie wanted to take him away from her."

He shook his head, wondering if Alice had a supply of sleeping tablets in her bedside table. Doreen looked at his worried face.

"Well, darling, cheer up, it's all right now!"

"For the moment," Reg Sugden said. "Touch wood—for the moment."

Later Doreen told her office room-mate that men were fascinating. "Boorish old north country Reg has learnt far more about women than Froggie Ducane, in spite of Froggie's absolutely *super* brain, darling!" she said, knowing little or nothing of Rachel Levin or what Sugden had learnt, or the high cost of it.

CHAPTER 4

Alice Robins went back to her bed-sitting room and packed a suitcase, the battle with Ducane almost forgotten. She was only aware that her world had suddenly been turned upside down, that everything was in a state of flux. Only one fact was certain: Alexi had defected and would not be going back to Russia—if he could help it. The happy development was hedged round with peril. Ducane might be right in his belief that fratricidal warfare had broken out between the KGB and the GRU, or he might not. One undisputable fact was that both branches of Russian Intelligence would probably be united about one thing: Alexis Ivanovich Schorin would have to be killed, or kidnapped and smuggled back to Moscow.

There might even be rivalry as to who would be able to claim the distinction of killing him. He would have to leave the country, of course, that was certain. All she knew was that wherever he went she would go with him so long as he needed her.

A sickening thought made her blink. The time might come when he would want to say, "Well, it was nice while it lasted." He was so volatile and unpredictable that she knew speculation was useless.

She paid her landlady two months' rent in advance. Then she lugged her big suitcase downstairs, picked up a taxi in Kensington High Street, and drove to the Safe House which wasn't a house at all but a flat near Blackfriars Bridge, overlooking the Thames, which Ducane rented for occasions like the present one. Ducane often wondered how safe it was. But it was the best he could do with the funds available.

Alexi Schorin was waiting for her, standing by the window, looking out at the Thames below, two big suitcases by his side.

Ducane was also by his side. They both turned and greeted her. Schorin was pale and gave her a thin smile. Then he shouted at Ducane.

"Ask me questions, go on, ask me questions. Before it is too late!"

"We'll ask you questions all right," Ducane murmured. "Not now, later. When you are out of London, safe."

"I shall never be safe! Ask me questions now!"

Alice's heart sank. She knew the mood he was in. He was like a wild animal caught in a net, lashing out, impervious to reason.

She guessed what was still going on in Ducane's mind. Was Alexi Schorin a genuine defector, or an expensive plant, a GRU gamble which, despite the price to be paid in lives, could provide fabulous results for the future? Was the GRU really at war with the KGB? Was the shooting of poor Yuri part of the price, the dressing tossed in it to make the dish more palatable? Was Schorin genuine when he had said that if he fully defected he would be doing it for her? If so, his hand had been forced, the pace accelerated. Or was the whole thing, even the death of a fellow GRU officer, an elaborate set up? So many questions, so few answers. Indeed no answers at all. She saw Ducane looking at her thoughtfully. As if answering some of her questions he took her aside and whispered:

"The balance of trade is on our side, Alice. That's the test, that's always the yardstick. Credit side—we have names and addresses. Not a lot, but some. Debit side: names of one or two of our officers, and a secretary, you—and the location of a Safe House, if you can call it that. Probably all just confirmation of what they knew already. Assessment: profit to us—up to now," he said aloud.

"Ask questions and you'll have more profit," Schorin shouted.

"Later," Ducane said abruptly, and took a piece of paper out of his pocket and gave it to Alice. She read: Number 3 The Almshouses, Melford, Melfordshire, and looked at Ducane inquiringly.

"Two bedrooms upstairs. For you and Alexis. One living-room downstairs, where your guru will sleep on a camp bed. All modern cons. Purely temporary, till we find something else."

"Guru?" She looked puzzled.

"Or keeper, if you like, guide, philosopher, friend, and protector—Reg Sugden. He'll meet you down there. He's furious. Hates camp beds."

Ducane looked at his wrist-watch. "You might as well go. Good luck. Nice day for a—"

Schorin interrupted. "Got the cassette, Alice?"

Alice nodded. Ducane looked puzzled.

"Ukrainian folk songs, Alexi asked me to keep it for him."

"I want the cassette kept safe. In case I feel lonesome. And I want Alice to have it as a souvenir, in case—"

"In case what?" Ducane asked unnecessarily.

Schorin glowered at Ducane. "In case nothing," he muttered.

"Got your car?" Ducane asked. Alice shook her head. "It's in dock."

"Doesn't matter. There's a Dolomite outside. Like yours, but blue. Registration GHX 249M. False plate, of course." He picked up Alice's suitcases, moved towards the door, then stopped.

"The cassette will be safer with me, Alice dear."

"I want it with me," Schorin objected.

"I'll return it when you are settled in permanently."

"It is mine, and I want it with me," Schorin insisted. Ducane shook his head.

"It's *mine*, Alexi, all that you have is mine, you are mine, too, until I have you made a British subject and get you out of the country. Mine, Alexi, you are mine. But I take good care of my possessions."

Alice opened a suitcase, fumbled among some underclothes, took out the cassette and handed it to Ducane. Schorin watched her. Before she finally closed the suitcase she caught his eye.

"I had to do it, Alexi," she whispered.

Ducane sighed. She seemed a sad case, far gone, but it couldn't be helped, one had to cope with the situation as it was. He carried her bag out to the lift for her, and handed her a bulging white envelope. "£200 advance expenses," he said, "Reg has more when and if required."

He kissed her lightly on the cheek. "Take care, Alice. Reg will look after you. Try and keep this young man happy, he'll need you."

Ducane felt Schorin's hand on his shoulder.

"Where is Melford?" Schorin asked, suspicion in his eyes.

"A small country town about ninety miles from London. You will be safe there if you act reasonably."

"Safe?" Ducane heard Alexi Schorin laugh scornfully. "And almshouses, what are these almshouses?"

"Almshouses are houses built by charitable persons for poor and distressed people. In Melford the almshouses were to provide homes for the widows of naval officers. Built in 1820. Five houses, modernised now, of course. One or two are vacant, because there aren't many naval widows in Melford."

Schorin put down his suitcases and flushed. "So! I am to live in a poor person's house! Promises promises! Yes, of *course* you will have high rank, have a fine office, good salary, do important work! And now what?" he shouted.

He picked up his suitcases and strode into the lift. Ducane handed the car keys to Alice.

"Good luck—you'll need it, one way and another." He glanced briefly at Schorin and then at Alice and grimaced.

She took the A40-M40 route via Woodstock. For much of the time she had noted a big black car, possibly a Rover, a couple of hundred yards behind her. Sometimes she lost sight of it, when one or two cars overtook it and cut in behind her. Normally it annoyed her to have cars following too closely behind, but today she welcomed them, because the black car worried her.

Thinking to shake it off she pulled in at an automatic car wash. While awaiting her turn two cars pulled in behind her. Then, as she was drawn past the giant whirling brushes, she caught a glimpse of the black Rover's bonnet nosing into the queue. In the dark throbbing womb of the car wash with its enormous brushes and octopus-like polishing tentacles she felt warm and secure and was sorry when at the far end the green light signalled to her to switch on her engine and take to the road again; and she wondered briefly whether her future life would be one of glancing uneasily into driving mirrors, afraid of what might be behind her.

Two miles outside Woodstock, at the Duke of Marlborough public house, she swung left and took the road which would lead to Charlbury, Chedlington and eventually to hilly Burford and beyond. She put on speed but was no match for the sleek Rover. Beyond Charlbury, instead of taking the road to Chedlington she continued straight on.

"There's a Rover following us," she said abruptly.

"I know that," Schorin said equally abruptly, and took an automatic out of his shoulder holster and laid it on his lap. She felt suddenly queasy.

"Don't use that, it'd lead to complications."

"It could lead to other complications if I don't. Ducane will have to sort them out."

All the journey he had been sulky, only occasionally breaking the silence with disgruntled remarks. But now, as he fondled the automatic on his lap, his voice was strong and firm, as if he exulted at the prospect of action.

"It's part of Ducane's job—to sort things out for me."

Her heart sank. "It's not as easy as that over here, in this country."

"Then it's too bad for Ducane, isn't it?"

She shook her head, but said nothing, wondering if he would ever come to terms with the power difference between a citizen in Britain and a KGB or GRU officer in Russia. The incongruity of a dangerous animal with an automatic and the mellow honey coloured houses appalled her. In Charlbury she was tempted to pull up at the Bell Hotel and take him inside. But she knew it would only be a delaying action. They couldn't stay inside for ever. There had to be an end, and the end came a few miles further on.

A herd of cows was spread across the road, approaching them in a slow, indolent way, one or two lolloping forward a yard or two, others stopping for a quick snack at roadside grass. The black Rover drew up alongside her, and she saw with a feeling of numb resignation that it had darkened one-way vision windows, so that those inside could see out, but those outside could not see in. She watched, sitting still and feeling hopeless as one of the windows was quickly lowered, and she felt Schorin move, so that her head-rest came between him and whoever was in the black car. She herself leaned forward so that the steering wheel covered the right side of her face, and lowered her own window, thinking that a bullet might miss her head, but that shattered glass could damage her face and still leave a hole in the window for subsequent bullets.

She was conscious of the hard metal of Schorin's gun pressing against her left shoulder blade and was wondering what the lad with the cows would do in the seconds ahead when she heard a voice say in a flat tone:

"You're taking your curves too fast, lass, you want to take it more steady on these winding roads, you do an' all."

"I could kill you, Reg," she shouted in a voice nearly hysterical with relief, "following us like that!"

"Aye, well if I don't somebody else might kill *you*," Sugden said, and let in his clutch and began slowly to nose his way through the rest of the cows. Then he stopped and let Alice and Schorin pass.

In Burford she pulled up at the top of the hill and bought an evening paper, glanced at the headlines and the opening paragraphs on the front page, and handed the paper to Schorin, and drove on.

"Bastards, KGB bastards," muttered Schorin. The headlines were inevitably big, but hard facts were scanty:

RUSSIAN DIPLOMAT SHOT IN PHONE BOX
Soviet Embassy Protest

A Soviet diplomat visiting London for the RAF Air Show was shot and killed in a telephone box in the early hours of this morning. Scotland Yard's anti-terrorist squad is investigating. The Soviet Embassy has sent a strongly worded protest to the Foreign Office demanding better protection for Soviet representatives, both those here already, and those visiting these shores.

An embassy spokesman said: "It is intolerable that bona fide Soviet citizens enjoying the hospitality of this country should not receive adequate protection. There is little doubt that this is the work of a criminal group of Trotskyist or anarchist degenerates sheltering in this country under the guise of political refugees. It is possible that this crime may be the work of imperialist Tsarist White Guard assassins, but that is unlikely. Few of them remain, and they are now very aged."

Alice glanced quickly sideways at Schorin and was dismayed by the light of battle in his eyes.

"How long will it be before this froglike Ducane leaks the news of my—" He stopped, still baulking at the word defection.

"Maybe two or three days, maybe longer, if possible. And then perhaps only confirmation of information leaked by your former—"

"My former colleagues in the GRU. Oh, no, little Alice, not them, they will not leak it. But the bloody KGB might."

She could not decide who Alexi disliked more, the KGB or what he called "Brezhnev and his gang." The KGB were Brezhnev supporters. They had at their disposal the greater part of the funds available. Unlimited expenses, some of which could be creamed off for expensive presents for their wives, jewellery, furs, scent, silk stockings, luxury soaps and other Western products in short supply in Russia. No wonder they were Brezhnev men. KGB wives were happy, GRU wives were bitter. She had heard about it all when she was Ducane's secretary. Long ago.

Melfordshire no longer existed. Alice knew that. During its thousand years' life it had lain undisturbed, and content with its lot, about twenty minutes' drive north of where the borders of Oxfordshire, Worcestershire, and Gloucestershire often met and parted, each going its own sleepy way. Then, to the surprise and disgust of Melfordshire citizens, they woke up one morning and discovered that a Conservative government, elected as most thought to conserve them, had ceased to do so. Not only had it failed to do so, it had taken positive action to de-conserve them. Melfordshire was wiped from the face of all new Ordinance Survey maps.

But the county town of Melford, with its cathedral, was graciously permitted to live and even expand and modernise, with a shopping precinct for pedestrians and a system of one-way streets guaranteed to bewilder all drivers arriving in the town for the first time.

Having inquired the whereabouts of the almshouses, she eventually found them, tucked away by the south side of the cathedral. She breathed a sigh of relief because at least she could park freely in front of them. They were in a row, detached one from another. In front of the middle one was a notice carved into stout oak:

TO THE GREATER GLORY OF GOD AND TWELVE POOR WIDOWS OF SERVING OFFICERS DR. WILLIAM ANGLESON GENEROUSLY DEDICATED THIS EDIFICE IN A.D. 1820 OUT OF PIETY AND CHRISTIAN CHARITY. A faded notice underneath stated that in 1848 alterations had been made, and the former large building converted into several separate ones, though "preserving as much as possible the original character and stonework."

Alexis Schorin sniffed disdainfully. "Keeping twelve poor widows happy in one building is a problem which even Moscow has not yet solved."

Almshouse Number 3 was at the end of the row, a small squat building made of mellow local stone. They sat in the car for a few minutes looking at it.

"I hope the plumbing has been changed since 1820." Alexi Schorin said nothing. He was reading a notice stuck on the front window which said: Melford and District Rural Folk Song Society (Temporary Headquarters). Alice guessed Sugden had put it there.

"When can I have the Ukrainian folk song cassette back?" Schorin said suddenly.

"When Ducane has finished with it."

"When will that be? I want it now."

She was dismayed by his peremptory tone, and put a hand

on his forearm. "Alexi, dearest, you must try to reconcile yourself to some things."

"What things?"

"For one thing, dear love, your position is not what it used to be. Everybody will try to make you happy, and protect you, but you are no longer a KGB or GRU officer, a man of power, a person to be feared, a man to give orders."

"Why didn't they ask me questions? Why did they waste time? How long have I to live? Why waste time?"

"They will ask questions. It was all so sudden."

"When will my naturalization papers be given to me?"

"As soon as possible. It takes time."

"Time, time, always time being wasted!"

"You will have to change your name, of course."

He nodded and said gloomily: "Of course. Naturally. So I cease to exist! No country. No home except a miserable house built for a poor widow. And no name. A non-person."

His voice rose to the ranting pitch she dreaded. She glanced round, fearful lest anybody should overhear him. "We will think of a name, what shall it be? Perhaps something Scandinavian, because your accent is perfect but you sometimes make little mistakes in grammar."

"Mistakes, yes, I make mistakes!" He laughed ruefully. Then suddenly his voice dropped to his soft wheedling tone. He put a hand on each of her shoulders.

"I am here because of you, little Alice." She peered up at him through her glasses with the enormous lenses. A warm wave of love and protectiveness surged through her, making her heart beat faster. For a few seconds she allowed herself to luxuriate in the caressing warmth of his words. But like cold water came the memory of the transcripts of the telephone talk he had had with his friend. Was it hardly more than twelve hours since Yuri had given him the alarming news of his recall to Moscow, and been killed? She looked again into his blue eyes, sometimes cold, or angry, or impatient, but now so tender. Was he really here because of her? Or because he was afraid to respond to the summons from Moscow?

If she had agreed to go with him, would he have obeyed the

order and risked a deadly reception? Was it a coincidence that Yuri's first phone call had been followed by Alexi's plea to her? Was it all a ploy? Or was it a last desperate attempt to salvage his career? The only certainty was that they were together now; and jointly and severally, as lawyers say, they had to survive.

A loud voice interrupted her thoughts. "Well, are you coming in or are you going to stay there rabbiting?" Jerking her head round, she saw Reg Sugden standing in the doorway of Almshouse Number 3.

"Coming!" She smiled up at Schorin and led the way in.

There was, of course, no food in the house. She expected that. She made out a list for the following morning's shopping: bread, milk, butter, cheese, chops, cabbage, potatoes, eggs and bacon.

They ate out that evening and that same evening Superintendent Brock made his daily entry in his diary. He usually did it the following morning. But he felt a need to jot things down at once, to get facts and impressions right, before the situation was enveloped in turmoil and complications as he feared it would. Jane watched him as he wrote in his careful neat style:

ACC called me in. Angry, but that's normal. He said an important Russian visitor had been shot in London. And a Russian Intelligence defector is coming down here. He thought the two might be connected. The defector needed protection. Whitehall request. I made it very clear that I could not afford full protection since I had not enough officers. He saw my point, but said we must do our best.

CHAPTER 5

The following morning the comparative peace of the Melford traffic-free shopping precinct was welcome. And the thought of the Almshouse, slumbering in the shadow of the great cathedral, was soothing.

Alice turned out of the shopping precinct and made her way along Sheep Street. At the end of the street, taking her direction from a brief glimpse of the cathedral spire she turned left towards Cathedral Close.

She stopped abruptly, nearly colliding with a ghost from the past, Sam Letts, journalist, friend of all the world; and especially, after Pat had left her, the friend of Alice Robins.

The meeting produced in Alice both pleasure and panic. The feeling was laced with a streak of guilt. She had often felt it, recognised it, and even given it a nickname. She called the guilt the Sugden Syndrome. There had been a time when she would have paid good money to see Sam Letts every day. She sometimes thought that Pat himself would have contributed money for the same purpose, for she knew Pat quite liked her. The only trouble was that he had found somebody he liked even better and nipped off with the lady.

She had met Sam at an advertising agency party to which the press had been invited to publicise some new Wonder Washing Powder. Ironically, Pat had introduced Sam to her, and, with his own private treason in mind, was doubtless glad that they obviously got on so well. Later they had many good times together. Sam drank a bit but not more than many journalists. She could have married Sam Letts, had she wished. She knew that. Admittedly on the rebound, but she guessed they would have been happy. A rebound is better than no bounce.

He was in his late thirties, a stocky man, with grey blue eyes, a healthy complexion despite the whisky, a pleasant face, dry humour, and a temperament which was never ruffled. They kissed a good deal but it never went further than that. His wife Joan, like many north country wives, had not transplanted well when he migrated south to Fleet Street; yet she was a good wife, loyal and affectionate, but Alice was not surprised when one day, after a country picnic, Sam had looked at her and said in his north country voice, "Alice, shall I ditch Joan? She could go back north, she's never been really happy in the south."

She had shaken her head. "Oh, Sam, Sam, I could never wish on any woman what I went through." She had softened her words with a long kiss. He had not argued with her. All he had said in his flat voice was: "Well, I shall always love you, remember that."

Soon after, he had got a job as a news agency correspondent in Paris and Joan had gone with him. Three years later Sam, back in London, had telephoned.

There was the usual exchange of surprised pleasantries. He wanted to see her. How about dinner? Well, no, she had a dinner date. Just a quick drink before dinner? All right, just a very quick one. Royal Court Hotel, Sloane Square? Insofar as his pleasant but dull voice could ever reflect excitement it did so when he had telephoned her that evening after his arrival on holiday from Paris.

Now, facing him unexpectedly in Melford, the memory of that last meeting in the Royal Court Hotel flashed from the hiding place in her mind to which for emotional peace she had tried to relegate it for always. Disjointed sentences and impressions cruelly clawed their way up, each with a painful edge only partly dulled by the passing of time. Sam's blue-grey eyes, sometimes showing cynical amusement, but more often looking at her with tenderness. Sam saying with as much pleasure and excitement as he could ever permit himself, "She's left me." "Who, Joan?" "Gone back north! Couldn't stand the pressure of Paris. Did my best, but no go. She's fallen for the wealthy son of a textile mill owner who got out before prices slumped. She wants a divorce."

Sam took a big gulp of whisky. And she a slug of Bloody

Mary: vodka, Alexi's drink. Sam saying, "I'm free now! I still love you." *Alice, are you listening, I still love you! I love you, are you listening?*

What had her face portrayed, what expression had been in her eyes to make him repeat himself in such a dismayed tone? There had been no need to reply. Alexi had joined them.

She had not expected Alexi for another hour or more, had not anticipated what had happened, and had thought she could get rid of Sam in half an hour.

Alexi had arrived with an evening paper, having nothing else to do. He was holding a glass of vodka and ice and water, and had greeted Alice in his softest voice and sat down at their table uninvited. She introduced them.

"Sam's a newspaperman," she told Alexi.

"Alexis is a diplomat or something," she told Sam. "Soviet Embassy." It had all been years before Alexi had defected—in the period when life had been simple.

Then there was some uneasy desultory conversation. Noise and laughter from the adjoining bar. Both men casting covert glances at each other. Alexi in an extrovert mood. Sam looking somehow shrunken, watching Alexi, but above all watching her when she looked at Alexi. Then the crunch.

Sam Letts saying to her, "What about dinner next week?" And her reply: "I'm a bit tied up next week, Sam."

"Lunch?" A look of desperation in his eyes as he searched her face for any indication that she might relent.

"I don't get much time for lunch. Just a sandwich and a cup of coffee at my desk."

"I understand."

Sam had torn a leaf from his notebook, scribbled a telephone number on it. "Give me a ring if you can manage something."

She supposed she still had the scrap of paper in the clobber she had moved from her former London digs, unused, and still neatly folded as Sam had folded it when he handed it to her. He had muttered something she could not hear, and had strolled slowly out of the hotel. And out of her life, she had thought.

Alexis Schorin had gazed after him.

"That is a nice man, but he will—what do you say?—get no better?"

"Deteriorate. Run to seed."

Yet he was my friend, faithful and true to me when I needed him, she had thought miserably, as she watched Sam push his way through the hotel swing doors without a backward glance, a beaten man.

As Alice gazed beyond Sam Letts and saw the spire of the cathedral rising into the blue sky, her main emotion was fear and the knowledge that Sam was a newspaperman who had previously met Alexi. When the news of the defection was broken in the press Sam would certainly wish to meet him again.

"Sam, dear, what are you doing in this dump?"

"Looking for a story. Some rumour of pornography among town councillors. I'm freelancing."

"Thought you were in Paris, Sam?"

"Paris? Oh, Paris packed up, or rather packed me up. Soon after—"

"Soon after when?"

"Soon after—well, soon after we last met."

He shifted uneasily on his feet. He had deteriorated as Alexi had said he would. Eyes watery and a little bloodshot. Complexion blotchy. Stomach grown paunchy. Hand trembly when he raised a cigarette to his lips. Dear, kind Sam, was she the cause of it?

"And you, what are *you* doing here?"

She affected not to hear his question, and smiled and picked up her shopping bag.

"And what *are* you doing here, Alice?" he asked again.

"Living here, at the moment. In one of the almshouses. Just for a few days. A friend fixed it up."

He nodded and took the shopping bag from her.

"I'll walk back with you."

"You don't need to, Sam. It's not far."

"I know. Not far enough. You can't deny me this, at least. I still love you, you know."

At first she had resisted when he took the shopping bag, but short of a tussle in public she had to let him have it. She could smell whisky on his breath. He was probably in a mood to be obstinate, and she did not wish to be involved in a scene. It was better to humour him. They took a short cut through the shopping precinct. Sam Letts did not stagger, but he walked uncertainly and with care. At one point he stopped and put down the shopping bag.

"Married?" It was a direct question. She felt her heart beat faster. The question, spoken in his usual unemotional tone, floated softly on the air in the comparative quiet of the precinct, but she knew it was heavily weighted with trouble. Not for the present, but for the future. She tried to sidestep it.

"I hope to be. Soon."

"Shacked up with somebody?" She hated the expression and winced mentally.

"I suppose you could call it that."

He picked up the shopping bag again and they moved on.

"That Russian I suppose?"

Journalists ask questions easily. Questions trip off their tongues automatically, it's not rude inquisitiveness, it's a *deformation professionelle,* or so Pat, her advertising agent ex-husband had once told her years ago.

"Do you still call yourself Alice Robins?"

"Larsen, Alice Larsen. His full names are Alexis Hans Larsen. His mother's English, father Swedish.

"No," Sam Letts said with a smile. "His names are Alexis Ivanovich Schorin. I'm not likely to forget, am I? Not after that time in the Royal Court. That's the sort of meeting a man never forgets. Anyway, it is all in the morning papers, plus a picture, though it's a bad one." She made no comment, but quickened her step. Sam Letts, burdened with the shopping basket, puffed wheezily as he struggled to keep up with her. When they reached the almshouse she saw the notice still in the window of Number 3 and said, "He's compiling a book of international folk songs, folk songs of all the nations." She was extemporising feverishly. She and Alexi and Sugden had discussed what his name would be when he was naturalized and came out of purdah, but they had come to no decision as yet. Well, he was stuck with Alex Hans Larsen now, whether he liked it or not. And whether Sugden or Ducane liked it or not. Sugden had departed for a meeting with Ducane and As-

sistant Chief Constable Tomkins and she and Alexis Ivanovich Schorin, alias, Larsen, were on their own.

She took the shopping bag from Sam Letts and thanked him
and said goodbye, making no mention of a further meeting. It
was the last thing she wanted. Sam said hopefully:

"I'm staying at the Blue Boar if you want to get in touch."

"Maybe we might have a coffee one day," she said, not
meaning it, and Sam, guessing she didn't mean it, said, "That
would be great." He was turning away with a hurt look in his
eyes which shocked her when the door of Almshouse Number 3
opened, and Alexis Schorin dressed in a brown jacket and
grey slacks, stood in the doorway and shouted: "Who's your
boyfriend, bring him in, bring him into our bloddy pub! The
Alms House Arms! Drinks on the house, all guests welcome,
all tastes catered for!" He was in one of his exuberant, boyish
moods, confident and carefree.

Sam stopped and stared thoughtfully at the tall strong figure.
The noonday whisky fumes had cleared from his brain. As he
had said, no man forgets the face of somebody who has stolen
his woman. The plans evolved by Ducane, Sugden, and herself,
and approved by Alexi, the elaborate machinery for creating a
new personality were all at risk. The careful, step by step vet-
ting and security testing of each necessary link in the chain, so
that each could stand up to hostile scrutiny, were nearly com-
pleted, though not quite. Soon there would be a false birth
certificate for Alexander Hans Larsen; National Security and
National Health registration; naturalization papers; a passport
for Alexander Hans Larsen, profession, writer, a new life in a
far away country for Alexander and Alice Larsen. Little now
remained except some simple facial surgery and dyed hair, for
the passport photograph, if there was time. They could not
change the colour of his eyes. The rest was nearly ready, the
stage set for the birth of a new British citizen. Now what?

She wondered if he would ever learn to conquer his sponta-
neous, dangerous instincts. Probably not. She would have to
learn to live with it. Provided they both lived long enough to
learn to live with it. She heard Alexi shouting: "Come on in,
my little ones! A quick vodka before lunch! I brought some
with me—a wise precaution." Sam smiled at Alice.

"I would like to meet him again. He must have something I haven't got, including a small fortune."

She pretended to look surprised. "Oh, no, he hasn't got a fortune, big or small."

"He has, you know, if he plays things right. I can help him."

He pulled a folded newspaper out of his pocket and showed the front page to Alice. She heard Alexi shouting his invitation again, but ignored him. She was staring horrified at Sam Letts, first, then at the crumpled newspaper and the glaring head-lines:

RUSSIAN DIPLOMAT DISAPPEARS—ANOTHER IS SHOT
Man with Many Secrets?

It was all there. Alexi's name, his minor diplomatic post, the speculation that he was a spy, the bald statement that all Rus-sian diplomats are connected in one way or another with the KGB. No mention of the GRU. That would annoy Alexi, she thought briefly, and heard him calling again, impatiently. And at the end of the paragraphs the speculation that Alexi had sought political asylum in the West. Still holding the newspa-per, she followed Sam into the almshouse.

"This is Sam Letts, a newspaperman. This is Alex Larsen," she said, looking Alexi straight in the face. She knew instinc-tively that the ploy was hopeless.

"A man's entitled to change his name if he wishes," Sam said slowly. "We have met before."

Schorin's blue eyes were expressionless.

"Sam's a newspaperman," Alice said again brightly. Schorin turned and poured out drinks. Cinzano Bianco for Alice, whisky for Sam, vodka and ice for himself. Sam raised his glass to Schorin.

"Good health, Schorin. You'll need it."

"So will you," murmured Schorin, blue eyes cold and thoughtful.

"I'd have thought you'd have been out of the country by now," Sam Letts said.

"So did I." Schorin's eyes rested momentarily on Alice. He knew she was not responsible for the delay in producing the necessary documents to prove he was a British subject. But she was part of the system. As such she had to bear part of his resentment.

Abruptly, with north country frankness amounting to a lack of finesse that bordered on brutality, Sam Letts came to the point.

"I got some redundancy cash. Most of it's gone. I'm a freelance. We could clean up on this." He pointed to the newspaper and its headlines. "Every newspaper in the country will be anxious to buy a story about you. And every publisher a book: 'My Story,' by Alexis Ivanovich Schorin. 'Soviet Spy Tells All.' Thousand pounds an article. Five articles. Fifty thousand advance royalties for the book. 'Early Boyhood Years. My Days With The Russian Secret Service.' 'Why I Defected,' 'How I Defected,' 'My Plans and Hopes,' 'How Russia's Secret Service Works.' 'The Hidden Peril: Traitors Within.' All that."

Sam's tongue had been loosened by Schorin's whisky. He had sobered up from some morning drinking by the time he arrived at the almshouse but the alcohol still lurked in his blood, ready to be activated by just one drink. And Schorin had poured out a strong one for him.

"Fifty-fifty split between us. Sixty-forty, if you insist, sixty to you, forty per cent to me. Television rights, film rights, American rights, world rights." Sam Letts prattled on happily. Schorin went the rounds again, filling up the glasses, saying nothing till Sam had stopped his day-dream rambling.

"The frogman Ducane will pay me, he promised me all the money I need. I want a quiet life with Alice, I don't need money."

Alice looked at him with glowing eyes and smiled.

"I don't need money," he said again, more firmly.

Sam looked at him pityingly. "You will one day, when you are maybe on the other side of the world, you will, mark my words. Anyway, when my redundancy money is gone, I'll need it all right, and so will you in the end."

Schorin carefully put down his glass on a small side-table. The threat in Sam's words was veiled, but Schorin recognised it for what it was. He remembered a remark by his first boss in the GRU: "Always remember this, Alexis Ivanovich Schorin—most men will do anything for survival. And most women," he had added. They had been munching warm bread and schmalz and gulping vodka after a glorious ski run in the woods. It had been during the early days, long past, when his naval training was over, his GRU career beginning, and life had seemed a splendid adventure.

Instinctively, unconsciously, his GRU training guided him now. He looked at Sam Letts thoughtfully. The man had deteriorated, as he had predicted that he would. So much the better. Drink would kill him in the end via his liver. But not soon enough. He had nothing against Sam Letts personally. He was just a mortal threat.

His training had taught him that there are more ways of dealing with a threat than by direct confrontation. He pretended to hesitate.

"There is a great deal of talking to be done before I say yes or no, Sam. You permit me to call you Sam?"

"Certainly, Alexi," replied Sam happily.

"I'm afraid I haven't enough grub in the house to invite you to lunch," Alice said pointedly. Sam struggled to his feet.

"Give me a ring at the Blue Boar," he said. "Thanks for the drink." He gazed round at them, nodded, and walked carefully to the door and down the little untidy front-garden path. Once he stopped and unsteadily picked a white rose which he put in his buttonhole.

As Letts walked down the path Schorin watched him. His right hand groped for the automatic under his left shoulder, and he pulled it out. Alice, grey eyes wide with horror, flung herself at him and grabbed the automatic, and watched Sam fumbling with the latch on the garden gate.

"Stop it! Don't be a bloody fool!"

He looked at her, and followed the line of her gaze as Sam continued to fumble with the gate.

"Oh, him—I'm not a bloody fool, little Alice. There's more than one way of silencing a man."

"What way?" His eyes were expressionless and he did not reply.

Not a fool, she thought; but volatile. Would she wake up

one morning and wish for a month of total boredom, as Ducane did? Or a week of boredom? Or even just one morning when she could think: peace, perfect peace, what can I do today to fill in the time? Watching Schorin as he examined the magazine from his automatic and snapped it back, she momentarily conceded that such a wish might occur to her.

"Never a dull moment," she murmured. "Not for a mouse which lives with a big cat." Could a mouse tame a tiger? She recalled the Aesop fable. Helping a lion to escape is one thing; taming it is another. But a mouse had to try.

Sam Letts had reached the pavement outside, and was walking slowly along where the cathedral spire showed above the town. He stopped once and must have thought they were watching him because he turned and waved, then continued on his slow way, head down, shoulders hunched. Suddenly he straightened up and began to walk briskly, and before he disappeared from view he waved again. But it was not the despondent drooping wave of a defeated man. It was a jaunty flick of the hand. Something had cheered him up, some streak of hope seemed to have pierced the whisky laden mist in his brain. Was it the sudden clear view of distant riches, shimmering and luring him on? All that was needed was a little more pressure on Schorin. More sales talk. Perhaps a threat, very veiled. Alice would be on his side. He had noted the friendly even affectionate way she had looked at him during the drinks at the almshouse.

His footsteps quickened still more. He looked up at the sun. It was a beautiful day in every way, and it called for another drink or two at the Blue Boar. And one to go with his sandwich.

Being a big spender at the bar, he had got to know the landlord, Tom Barker, very well after a couple of days. It was while munching his ham sandwich that Sam said: "This town's going to be in the news soon, Tom." The landlord was swabbing the bar counter, removing the beer stains with a dirty cloth.

"What, this dump in the news?" Tom Barker asked, his voice contemptuous.

"There's more going on here than meets the eye." Sam

beamed round knowingly at the little circle of regulars having their lunchtime pint. "More than that I am not permitted to reveal," he said, his voice heavy with significance. "But mark my words, Tom! Just mark my words!"

A man appropriately called Sandy Short, because he was short and sandy haired, a stone mason who had worked on cathedral repairs ever since he was an apprentice, gulped two mouthfuls of Melford Strong Ale. He had a grey complexion, and a mournful lined face as though some of the atmosphere and some of the dust from the stonework had lodged permanently in the folds of his skin.

"Shouldn't be surprised, shouldn't be at all surprised. There's something rum going on at the almshouses," Sandy Short said darkly. "I was talking about them almshouses to old Councillor Shingler. What goes on at the almshouses? I asked him, I did, I asked him straight out. There was a bit in the *Echo* about it, early racing edition, but they took it out for the later editions. Who's the Melfordshire Folk Song Society, I asked him?

"Folk coming and going all the time. 'Fly by nights, London folk,' Mrs. Sole at Number Five says. Or worse, she says. Know what? One of the cars has darkened windows, so's you can't see who's in it, she says. Honest folk don't mind being seen. There's none of 'em look like the widows of serving officers, she says. Something ought to be done about it."

There was a general murmur of approval. Sandy Short scratched the side of his face with a broken fingernail.

"Folks are saying they could be crooks, I told him."

"Drugs," suggested a bald headed man drinking whisky. "Drugs, they could be drug pushers."

"That's what I told him, but he says, no, oh no, a friend of Assistant Chief Constable Tomkins asked if some friends of his could just move in for a short while, and then move out. Very temporary, like. Unofficial. Folk Song people who tried to get their thing off the ground, but it didn't catch on. Winding up, he says, just wanted somewhere to roost while they did it, repaying all the annual subscriptions and that sort of thing. So he agreed. In the town's interests to help the ACC when possible, he said. Then off he went."

"Fishy," said the bald headed man drinking whisky. "That's what I'd call it. Fishy."

Sam Letts, trying to separate useful grain from boastful chaff, knew that he had in his possession a weapon which could rock them all back. He took his glass of whisky to a chair near a window. Now and again he glanced back at the drinkers by the bar. All gabby, all wrong. He, Sam Letts, former foreign correspondent, future best-seller writer, he knew the truth. In Fleet Street other newspapermen regarded him as a spent force. He knew that because they were always so polite when he met them. "Have a drink, old boy!" Too polite. It wasn't natural, born of kindliness, sired by professional sympathy, it was the kiss of death. Funds had been running low. The time could have come when he might not have wanted a drink, just something to eat and a bare floor to sleep on in somewhere warm and dry. Now, suddenly, the scene had changed, and he had a winner in his stable which, paradoxically, couldn't run yet. He still loved Alice, though the pain had gone. He was glad he had never quarrelled with her. Maybe one day she and the Russian might split. And she might need him again. It called for a third drink. He got up, fetched it, and sat down.

He heard Tom Barker shouting, "Last orders, gentlemen, please!" and subsequently the closing and locking of the pub doors, and the clink and clatter as glasses were collected and washed for the six o'clock opening. He rested an elbow on an arm of his chair, and his head on his right hand. The opening words of his story, which would show Fleet Street and the whole newspaper world that he was not a spent force, began to form in his mind. After the newspaper articles would come the book, the TV script, the film script. Instead of dreading the morning post he would look forward to it. He toyed a good deal with the opening sentence of the story he would write, but finally settled on a straightforward beginning:

Alexis Ivanovich Schorin, the Russian Secret Service defector, talked to me before he left this country for a secret hiding place abroad. With him was his pretty English girl friend, Alice. Both looked tense but happy.

Schorin said that although he loved Russia he had for

some years become increasingly disillusioned by the present Soviet regime to which he often referred as "Brezhnev and his corrupt gang." He admitted that although he admired the Western way of life, he hoped to be able to return to his homeland one day when the present regime had been overturned. To that end, he would assist Western Intelligence to the best of his ability.

"I realise there is a price on my head," he said. Outlining his life. . . .

Sam's thoughts came to a stop. He had no more material in his head. But that would come later. He heard a voice, Tom Barker's, say: "You might find it quieter in the residents' lounge, sir." He got up sleepily and walked to the lounge. On the way he suddenly appreciated clearly and clinically how completely he had Schorin in his power. Alice, too. Both of them. Schorin was on the run, in hiding, and Alice was with him, and he could tell from the way she still looked at Schorin that Schorin was her world. He didn't need to bargain with either of them for the rights in the articles or in the book or about TV or films. He could demand them, make his own terms. What terms? He had finally to settle that in his mind before he saw Schorin again. Sixty per cent to Schorin and forty per cent to himself was, on reflection, a little too generous.

After all, he would have to do the hard work, the writing, the negotiating, make the arrangements for Schorin to get his share discreetly, so that nobody could trace where the money went and thus get at Schorin. An assassinated Schorin would be of no use to anybody, certainly not to Sam Letts. Or to Alice, come to that. He was still very fond of Alice, he admitted to himself. He would take a sort of paternal interest in her welfare. Sixty per cent was too much for Schorin. All Schorin had to do was spout his head off while he, Sam, did the real work, and the haggling with editors and publishers; because he wasn't going to have a lousy literary agent sitting on his fat backside in London creaming off ten per cent, and another rogue abroad lopping off another ten per cent, while the tax man swiped thirty-three per cent of the rest or whatever he would demand.

An uneasy thought occurred to his bemused mind about TV

and film rights. He didn't know much about that world, so he might have to have an agent for those rights. Sam often told himself, and indeed others who were polite enough to listen, that it was as important to know what you could *not* do as to know what you *could* do.

But that was a matter for the future, the rosy future.

Fleet Street thought he was a spent force, but he wasn't, he was an old grey dog, with strong teeth, or an old grey fox, you could take your choice.

He heaved himself to his feet, and stood looking uncertainly towards the door which led to the residents' lounge. Tom Barker, the landlord, sleeves rolled up to show the tattoo marks on his brawny arms, made his way hastily towards him. It would be easier to guide him to the lounge than to carry him. Sam pointed at him as he approached.

"Look, Tom, old boy, if you can bear to hear the truth you've spoken twisted to make a trap for fools, or watch the things you gave your life to broken, and stoop and build 'em up with worn out tools, and force your heart and nerve and sinew to serve your turn long after they are gone, and so hold on, old boy, when there's nothing in you except the Will which says Hold on, yours is the earth, old boy. Dear old Kipling, more or less, good old Kipling."

"Maudlin, sloshed," thought Tom Barker. "If it comes to holding on it's a good job there's a few chairs for him to hold on to."

In the lounge Sam Letts sank gratefully into an easy chair. Now and again, before he fell asleep, he thought, "you might have waited, Alice," and a couple of self-pitying tears rolled down his cheeks. But next time it would be different. Soon any dame in the land would be glad to marry Sam Letts. Although his name would not be on the book, the secret would leak out. He would make sure of that. But could he find a doll he wanted to marry? Of course he could. Well, he supposed he could. The earth is yours and every thing that's in it. Good old Kipling.

Sam dozed away the afternoon, believing there was no hurry.

CHAPTER 6

Assistant Chief Constable Tomkins, two years previously, had had a conversation with Ducane which he was to regret. A good lunch with lavish doses of excellent wine had mellowed the ACC to the extent that his normally hostile and suspicious blue eyes looked merely expressionless. Had Ducane but known it, Tomkins was bordering dangerously on a feeling of friendly approval even for this curiously froglike creature from Whitehall.

In the ACC's view, most men from Whitehall were soppy Civil Servants or poofs or both. And whatever else he was, Ducane in the opinion of the ACC was no poof.

It was after the third port and second coffee that Ducane had tentatively broached the subject of accommodation which might be needed at some time in the future for "a friend." Despite his peppery manner, Tomkins was no fool. The time might come when the post of Chief Constable was up for grabs. A Whitehall friend with Home Office contacts might be useful. Expansive after good food and wine, and with his usual keen eye for what might be good for Tomkins, the ACC had airily replied that he could probably help. He knew the chairman of the Housing Committee, a Councillor Shingler. "He is also chairman of the Almshouses Committee. One may become vacant soon."

In the first weeks after Schorin had arrived in the almshouse, despite the endless questions and answers, he had been cooperative and cheerful. This was tiresome but normal. The position had improved by the beginning of the fourth week. Schorin was getting restive.

So was Ducane. He knew Schorin was holding something back, and Schorin knew he knew it. Moreover the chance meeting of Alice and Sam Letts held boundless possibilities for misfortune. The situation was most promising.

Two years had passed since the lunch. And by now any feelings of mild benevolence which Tomkins might have felt towards Ducane had evaporated like early morning mist. Forgotten, too, were his feelings of surprise and gratification when, each Christmas, he had received a case of malt whisky from Ducane as a gentle reminder of that rash lunch-time promise. Now Ducane had descended on him out of the blue with no more than a brief telephone call to announce his imminent arrival. Putting it baldly, and the irascible Assistant Chief Constable was an adept at putting things baldly as his officers knew to their discomfort, the Whitehall Frog had come to collect.

Glaring at the faces of the people seated in a semi-circle round his office desk, Tomkins felt like a bull in a Spanish arena. Short of offending the Whitehall amphibian there was no way out, but he intended to go down fighting.

"I'm not taking any responsibility for his safety."

"Haven't got the men, sir," Brock agreed. "Minimum routine protection is all we can manage."

"And I don't want any trouble if it can be avoided. Melford is a peaceful town," Tomkins said, looking anything but peaceful. "I want to keep it that way. I trust that is clear?"

"Of course," Ducane murmured.

"I don't give a dam' if the KGB and the GRU slit each other's throats so long as they don't do it in Melford."

"Nor do I," smiled Ducane.

"So long as it isn't Schorin's," Sugden said quickly when he heard Alice Robins gasp.

"That goes without saying," agreed Ducane.

"Aye, but it might as well be said," Sugden remarked. He had seen Alice's stricken face.

ACC Tomkins had scowled at them again. He now felt annoyed with Ducane. Ducane represented something he knew little or nothing about, and didn't wish to. In his view Intelligence stuff was a nuisance, involving a lot of hokey-pokey, and he wanted nothing to do with it. But he had not seen fit to go back on his promise to Ducane, nor forgotten the reason. One day, possibly soon, the post of Chief Constable would become vacant.

It was soon after five o'clock when Sam heard the voice of Tom Barker's wife, and felt her shaking him. "Mr. Letts, sir, Mr. Letts, there is a gent on the phone for you."

Sam Letts sat up and yawned. "Who is it, did he give a name?"

"Sounded like Arson, to me, Mr. Arson, hope he won't set the pub on fire." Betty Barker was a round, pink cheeked woman of about forty, who liked a childish joke.

"Larsen, Mr. Larsen, half Swedish," Sam explained patiently.

"I said you were resting, but I'd call you. You can use the extension in our office, if you like, Mr. Letts."

Sam thanked her and shambled into the office, and lifted the receiver. He was still half bemused by sleep, but not for long. Schorin was putting on one of his exuberant performances. How lucky to find Sam in! Did Sam know Melfordshire and the Cotswolds? No? Well, he himself did, it was part of his patrol in the old days.

"Alice has had a good idea, Sam."

"That's encouraging, what's her idea?"

It was encouraging in more ways than one. It showed that Schorin was at least not avoiding him. He might be softening. He listened to Schorin's eager voice. It was a beautiful evening, it was only five o'clock. He and Alice would pick him up in the car, drive up Gate Hill, past Gallows Point. Wonderful view from the top. Then on past Bullbrook, then along the south side of the River Mell to where it joined two other streams. Lovely little bridge, said to be Roman, but that was unlikely. Quite a nice short waterfall and a little whirlpool at the bottom of one of the streams, and other pools, too, some with trout, did Sam like fishing? No. Well, never mind, he didn't, either, but it was worth a visit. Then on and have dinner about eight o'clock in a nice little pub he knew. How about it? The words gushed out, sometimes in an overbearing tone which seemed to brook no opposition. Sometimes cajoling. Sometimes in a wheedling tone which it was hard to resist.

The more he had thought about it, the more Sam had realised that he had Schorin completely in his power. He didn't need to negotiate terms, he could impose them. But he wouldn't need to. Schorin would need the lolly later. For Alice, one way or another. To keep her—or leave to her in his will. Dear Alice. He would be fair. Fifty-fifty with this defector bloke.

"That'll be nice," he now said. "But I don't want to go late to bed."

"Neither do I," Schorin agreed.

I bet you don't, thought Sam acidly, with Alice in mind. But in the event all were in bed much later than they wished.

CHAPTER 7

Alice believed that there are some moments when even an insensitive soul is caught by beauty, and she was far from insensitive. It can happen in a trembling instant, and like a candle flame can be as quickly extinguished. A time when beauty lures the spirit into a false peace. This was an evening of tranquility. Hardly a leaf seemed to stir. In the cottage gardens along the winding lanes and in the villages roses clung to garden walls, clematis covered roofs, old hedges at garden gates had sprouted the scarlet and yellow flowers of nasturtiums. The sky was gilded by the sun, and above the golden haze was a gentle blue as if the day were reluctant to leave. On small green hills sheep were grazing. The words of the old hymn, "Sheep May Safely Graze," came into Alice's mind. On such an evening sheep might indeed safely graze. She saw some small boys leaning over the curved stone bridge they said was Roman, at the bottom of the hill where a river ran beside the railway line. Concentrated on their fishing they hardly noticed the coming of the car. They were listening intently to the sounds of the river flowing gently over the stones.

There were still moments when one could see a Constable painting come to life; but as suddenly as the picture had appeared the children were gone. Many of the verges had not yet been cut and were splashed with colour, the white of Queen Anne Lace, the blue of wild geraniums, the scarlet of poppies and the purple of loosestrife.

They drove into a village that had the quality of an old water colour. The church with its square tower had itself become a golden image.

But something was wrong that evening. It was not the company. An added pleasure was that Sam and Alexi seemed to be getting on well together, often discussing the condition of the world with mordant humour. So what was wrong? The position was no worse than during the past week. Different, but no worse. The air was warm and still it lacked the heaviness which could precede a gathering storm.

So she could not blame the weather for her mood of depression. Indeed depression was the wrong description of it. It was more a sensation of alertness, wariness, a tension which prevented her from relaxing and enjoying what should have been a happy outing. She refused to consider what she had heard described as Woman's Intuition. Trying to analyse her unease, she came to the conclusion that it was caused by the absence of Sugden, the Watchdog, as she called him. Learning that Sam Letts was going with them, the Watchdog had accepted a longstanding invitation to spend an evening with Brock in Sheldrake Drive. Sam Letts was far from being an effective Watchdog but as a newspaperman he was better than no deterrent at all. The KGB did not appreciate witnesses to an assassination. Sugden did not always accompany her and Alexi on shopping visits to the centre of Melford, feeling that nothing was likely to happen in the bustling streets, though Sergeant Bob Frost or Sergeant Wally Jones sometimes kept a discreet eye on them. Alice shared Sugden's views, but outside Melford, even on an evening like the present one, she felt like a crab without its protective shell.

At dinner in the delightful old inn to which Alexis Schorin drove them she contributed little or nothing to the conversation. She picked listlessly at her prawn cocktail and ate only one of the two tiny mutton chops, and a few mouthfuls of the salad, before putting down her knife and fork. The waiter approached her, solicitous, anxious to please.

"Are the chops not to madam's liking?"

She looked up at his worried face. A Mediterranean type. Italian perhaps. Or Greek. Even in the Cotswolds there lingered an English tendency to regard service as demeaning, something to be performed grudgingly, and it would probably be worse in Australia, if they got there. Latin types regarded service as a skilled art in which to take pride. She smiled at the waiter.

"The food is excellent and beautifully served, and the wine is good." Her heart was warmed by his appreciative expression. Compliments were obviously rare.

"Would madam perhaps like to try something else?"

"No, thank you. I'm afraid I'm not very hungry."

"What's up, Alice?" Sam asked in his flat voice. "Sickening for something, love?"

"I don't think so, but—" Her voice died away. Schorin broke the silence.

"In my country—" he began, but Sam cut him short.

"In your former country, lad, you mean in your former country?"

"Over there, an ordinary dinner may take three or four hours. People do not complain, they prefer it like that. Eating out is a social entertainment, a change, something to make last as long as possible. They do not like quick meals in restaurants."

The hovering waiter closed in on them. "Sweet, fruit, madam? A little cheese, gentlemen?"

Alice looked at her watch and shook her head. They had arrived late and were the last in the dining-room. At the far end of the room another waiter was ostentatiously tidying up the tables and chairs.

"I think we ought to be on our way."

"Coffee?" Schorin asked.

"Too late, Alexi. You know what coffee does to me. Anyway you've a long day with Ducane and Sugden tomorrow." Sam Letts flicked his eyes at her and then at Schorin. "Ducane and Sugden?"

"Just two friends from London."

Sam made a mental note of the names. Any friends of Schorin could be friends of Sam Letts. Maybe sometime he would ask Schorin about them. He offered to share the bill with Schorin, but Schorin would not let him.

"Plenty more where that came from, isn't there?" Alexi winked at Alice.

"I hope so," she said. "I only hope so."

It was eleven o'clock as they began to drop down Gate Hill and past Gallows Point. At one moment Schorin looked sideways at Alice: "You shouldn't have mentioned Ducane and Sugden's names in front of that waiter. He might have been—"

Sam Letts laughed. "And there might have been a microphone under the table, I suppose?"

Schorin stared solemnly at the road ahead. "As a matter of fact, there might have been, I booked a table in advance. But you will remember that when we arrived I found fault with it, and insisted on another table."

"You think of everything," Sam Letts said sleepily from the back of the car.

"I intend to survive. Survival is my hobby." Schorin's voice was hard. Alice shivered. She had diagnosed another cause of her unease. Sam Letts, drink sodden so much of the time, in desperate need of success and money, would always be a mortal danger to Alexi, and Alexi knew it.

She had seen the expression on his face that first morning when Sam had had a drink with them. She had, of course, been a fool to jump to the wrong conclusion when Alexi had taken out his automatic. "I'm not a bloody fool," Alexi had said scornfully when she showed her alarm. Alexi might gain Sam's confidence, lure him on, and then, when time and circumstances were right, secretly take deadly steps to survive. She was too grateful to Sam not to try to save him. How, she did not know.

Schorin interrupted her thoughts. "The table we moved to was in the centre of the room. You noticed that?"

Sam Letts grunted sleepily from the rear of the car. "Rum choice, Alexi, I'd have thought. Exposed all round."

Schorin laughed. "Never sit near the wainscot, Sam, Micky the Mike loves to hide in wainscoting, he says it's warm and safe. And remember how you used to read about people liking to sit with their backs to the wall? Never do that. Walls reflect sounds—like a voice. Always sit in the middle of the room, Sam." There was no response from Sam Letts.

"He's nodded off, little Alice, just when I was giving him good free advice."

"No, I haven't," came Sam's muffled voice. "You're quite a lad, aren't you?"

Down below, the town of Melford, with its scattering of

small streets, shops, and house lighting would have looked like any other country town were it not for the bright blue light which bathed the cathedral. The great church stood up, calm and serene, like a tall aristocratic old lady conscious of her well preserved figure and looks and the elegance of her clothes. Even Sam roused himself.

"Floodlighting. Rehearsing for this year's Sound-and-Light pageant. They do it every year to commemorate the Day of Expiation."

"Expiating what?" Alice asked.

"They fought on the wrong side in the Civil War, love. Cromwell's soldiers bashed the place to hell, to make Melford expiate its sins, they said, though what sins poor little Melford had to expiate, except fighting for the King, nobody seems to know. Anyway, it's good fun I'm told. Mock battle and surrender, and people dressed as soldiers swigging Melford Strong Ale late into the night."

"It's beautiful!" Schorin murmured unexpectedly, slowing down the car.

"Better than flood lighting the Moscow Lubianke Prison," Sam murmured. Schorin did not laugh, nor did Alice. They dropped down into the town at the same slow speed and picked up Sugden in Sheldrake Drive. On one side of Cathedral Close a uniformed police officer waved them down. Schorin drew into the side of the road.

"Not to worry," Alice said. "Sam's the only one who's been drinking much, and he's not driving."

The officer approached them at a leisurely pace, and Schorin wound down his window.

"Good evening, sir. Are you aware that your near-side parking light is not functioning?" He put his head into the car, and stared keenly at Schorin, nostrils twitching.

"I'm the only one who's been boozing properly," Sam Letts's alcohol laden breath drifted from the back of the car. He sounded happy and sleepily at peace with the world.

"I'm driving with dipped headlights," Schorin said equably.

"Quite right, sir. I just thought you'd like to know, sir." The officer withdrew his head, switched off his torch, and stood up straight. Schorin's eyes were not bloodshot, his speech was steady. There was no obvious reason to breathalise him. Even if there had been, Sugden would not have intervened. Schorin had to learn to adapt himself to the law.

"Goodnight, sir."

Schorin did not respond. He was staring fixedly in the direction of the almshouses, which stood in a little road of their own, set back from Cathedral Close. Some were hidden by taller buildings, but Numbers 2 and 3 protruded and were visible from the car.

"All quiet round here?" Schorin asked suddenly. The officer bent down and again put his head into the car.

"Any reason why it shouldn't be, sir?"

"No, not really, I suppose."

"It's a peaceful town, on the whole, sir. You live round here, sir?"

"Just staying here. Temporarily. At Almshouse Number Three," Schorin replied slowly, staring at Almshouse Number 3. "Were the curtains closed when we left, Alice?"

"I don't think so. It was still afternoon. Broad daylight. Why?"

"Well, they are closed now."

The officer followed the line of their gaze and stroked his chin. "Come to think of it, sir, if anybody had asked me I would have said you were at home and perhaps even in bed, sir. I would have said I saw you let yourself in with a friend. You seemed to have trouble opening the door, as if the key didn't fit proper, sir. But you got in all right in the end, except that—"

"Except that it wasn't me, and I'm not at home, and I'm not in bed."

"No, sir, I see that. Perhaps intruders, sir? Or was you expecting anybody?"

"Yes and no." Schorin's voice was curt. "Who are you?"

"PC Burns, sir, Melford Police, it's either yes or no, sir. Were you expecting anybody?"

"Not to my certain knowledge."

"Burglars, perhaps burglars," Sam Letts said from the back seat. "Skeleton keys, and all that?"

"Who'd want to burglar an almshouse built for a poor widow of a serving officer?" Schorin said bitterly.

"Perhaps I'd better come back with you, sir?"

"You don't need to." But the officer had already opened a back door of the car, and was clambering in. It was a tight fit as he lowered himself down gently between Sam Letts and Sugden. Alice turned her head and looked at Sugden. She caught his eye. He looked taut and strained, lips compressed, and returned her gaze without speaking. Schorin stopped outside the house, and switched off the engine.

"Is there a kitchen door, sir?"

"Yes."

"I'll go round and guard the back, sir. You gentlemen go in by the front door. Don't try and stop anybody if he's armed, sir. Let him be, we'll pick him up later. Him or them."

PC Burns tiptoed along the short path then ran towards the rear of the house. Schorin locked the car doors. He had taken a heavy torch from the car, and as they approached the house he felt under his left shoulder and brought out his automatic.

"You could be in trouble if the cop sees that," Sugden said. "That's an offensive weapon."

"I feel offensive."

He flashed his torch on the front door. "It's been forced. I suppose it was bound to happen."

He snapped the short stubby automatic to load it, and moved the safety catch to the firing position. Then he switched off the torch and pushed the others aside.

"Stand against the wall. Flat. Don't do anything, whatever happens. I'm going in."

"Don't, Alexi!" Alice whispered. "Let Sam get the cop, let the cop go in when he comes back."

"It's what he's paid for," agreed Sam, all sleepiness gone now.

"This is my fight," Alexis Schorin said in a rasping voice, "and it's hardly started. You stay with Alice," he nodded to Sugden.

As Schorin was about to open the door Sam Letts called out: "Stop! I'll go in, you cover me from behind!"

"Don't be bloddy silly, you're unfit," snapped Schorin. "Stay where you are."

He kicked the door open. Holding his torch in his left hand, as far from his body as possible, and bending low he charged into the house. In front the little staircase led steeply up to the bedrooms. He pushed open the kitchen door, flashed his torch round, then tiptoed to the living-room and turned on the light and peered cautiously round the door and went in. Behind him he heard Alice gasp, and Sam Letts mutter an obscene oath, as they stared at the devastation. Alice put a hand on Schorin's arm and pointed up at the ceiling with her other hand. A floorboard creaked. A few seconds later, as they listened, the noise was repeated.

"The bloddy man's upstairs!" Schorin rushed from the room. Halfway up the narrow staircase he stopped, pointed the beam of his torch at the top of the stairs, and shouted: "Come on out, come downstairs with your hands up, I've got a gun." The circle of light made by his torch on the landing wall was suddenly joined by another shaft from another torch.

"If you've got a gun in your hand drop it," Schorin called. "I say again, drop it. Let me hear it fall. Come down now! If you have a gun in your hand I'll fire, do you hear, I'll fire."

Schorin meant what he said. He heard footsteps approaching the landing at the top of the stairs, but there was no other sound, no thud of a gun dropping to the floor. He checked that the safety catch on his automatic was still in the firing position. As a last attempt to avoid a gun fight he repeated the warning in Russian. He remembered Yuri's death in the London phone box, and a wave of hatred against the KGB swept over him, drowning all other thoughts. He did not want the man to surrender peacefully. He wanted to kill him. Yuri had been a true friend, and Yuri would not be the first true friend he had avenged.

For Schorin all was darkness and mental turmoil until the beam of his torch rested on the startled and annoyed face of PC Burns, and was reflected in the metal Melford police badge on his helmet.

"I hear you all right, sir, and I don't like what I hear, sir."

Alice had switched on the hall light and was watching the

constable as he carefully followed Schorin down the stairs. At the bottom he looked Schorin up and down. Schorin had replaced his automatic in his shoulder holster.

"Are you a foreign gentleman, sir?"

"Yes, I am at the moment."

"He'll soon be a British citizen," Sugden said.

"Not if he goes around carrying things like I saw when I was coming down these stairs, sir. Or was I imagining things?" He scratched his chin thoughtfully. "Yes, maybe I was imagining something, sir." He winked heavily, radiating a friendly feeling for somebody under stress. He pointed upstairs towards the bedrooms.

"It's the same up there, sir, like as in the kitchen and living-room, things you'd think would have been nicked are still there. But it looks—" He broke off, as if in search of the right words. "Everything's smashed to smithereens," he finished lamely.

"Oh no!" Alice turned towards the living-room and all five of them walked into the room. Nothing was undamaged. The sofa had been disembowelled with a knife and the stuffing pulled out of it, so that it looked like an exaggerated picture of a body in a gruesome book of anatomy. The chairs were the same. The few books which Alice had brought with her had been torn apart. Even the prayer book which she had had on her first communion day, had been ripped. The roses she had carefully arranged in a jug had been thrown to the floor and the carpet was soaked with a brown stain. They went into the kitchen. The contents of the cupboards had been pulled out and smashed as if with a hammer. Coffee, tea bags, milk cartons, tins, everything was piled in the centre of the floor, and on top of the soggy mess was the broken kitchen table and some smashed chairs. In the bathroom which adjoined the kitchen the portable television set they had brought with them had been taken from the living-room and was in the bath which was half filled with water. The plastic lavatory tank had been ripped off the wall.

"Why isn't the place flooded?"

Sugden indicated the large stop cock on the wall. It said, "Mains Water," and the red hand pointed to "*off*."

"They didn't want to attract attention by flooding the place," said PC Burns.

Everywhere they looked, and everything they looked at, was destroyed. It was as if some extraordinary animal had carefully gone through everything, tearing, biting and stamping, in some sort of frenzy. Senseless destruction produces a feeling of helpless rage. With Alice it produced a feeling of deep sadness. She stepped over the destruction and went up the small staircase to the bedroom. It was the same story.

Torn sheets, clothes cut up, suitcases ripped apart and the linings pulled out. And here they had even smashed the large bottle of scent she had been given by Alexi. Verbena is a delicate scent but now it impregnated everything, adding a sickly odour of decay to the scene. She would never use that kind of scent again. She sat down on the bed and looked at the Victorian fireplace, a curved iron grate a foot or two from the floor. The remains of her cashmere jumper were still smouldering in it.

She went downstairs, numbed and horrified, and joined the others in the living-room. Sam Letts was wandering about the room, straightening pictures on the walls, including one or two which had had their glass smashed. PC Burns was writing in his notebook.

"How did you get in?" she asked him. He looked up.

"They left the back door open, maybe in case they wanted to do a quick getaway. Vandals, madam. Perhaps their excuse would be that you shouldn't be in an almshouse, them houses being built for other purposes. Maybe youngsters."

"We're only here for a short while," Alice explained, her voice trembling. "Assistant Chief Constable Tomkins fixed it with Councillor Shingler." PC Burns nodded and went on writing. Schorin was standing in the middle of the room, a piece of paper in his hand. Alice looked over his shoulder to see what he was reading. It was in cyrillic writing. Having no knowledge of Russian it meant nothing to her. PC Burns looked at Schorin. "Can you help, sir, give us a lead? Are you aware of anybody who might have a grudge against you, or against Mrs. Larsen?"

"Plenty. But they don't live in Melford."

PC Burns nodded again. "I will report that you know of no local inhabitants who might have cause to break into these premises and be guilty of widespread destruction therein, right?"

"Correct," said Schorin and Alice together. In response to her request Schorin handed her the piece of paper he had been holding.

"What's it say?" she asked.

"Nothing unexpected."

"What's it say?" she insisted. Schorin tore up the paper and threw the pieces into the wastepaper basket.

"It says this is just a beginning. Next time it will be you unless I go to the Embassy and say I wish to return to Moscow. It is written in—what do you say? Obscene language."

Schorin's blue eyes were thoughtful and sombre.

"What are you thinking about?" Alice asked uneasily.

"I was thinking that I ought to let the KGB win."

"What do you mean, Alexi?" There was a wild, panicky note in her voice.

"I ought to go back. Yes, I ought to."

Sam Letts said loudly, "Don't be plain, bloody daft, man!" Poor old Sam saw he was in danger of losing his meal-ticket for life, and for Sam, as Sam probably realised, there would never be another chance like it.

Schorin glanced at him. He said: "I came over to Ducane and London for Alice. Now I think I must go back to Brezhnev and Moscow for her."

Hopeless, hopeless, thought Alice, volatile and unpredictable, a child that needed a firm nanny. She heard Sam Letts laugh.

"'It's a far, far better thing that I do now than I've ever done before,' don't talk rubbish. That sort of thing is old hat nowadays."

"Not in—not where I come from. People are still patriotic, and loyal, willing to sacrifice themselves. Over there in—"

"In Sweden," interrupted Alice quickly.

"Over *here* you've got to look after Number One," mumbled Sam Letts, "and to hell with other people."

"Without Alice there would be no Number One. Alice is

dusha moya, my soul, she is *zadushevny,* even, the one behind the soul." Alexi Schorin spoke in a hoarse voice.

PC Burns looked up. It didn't sound like Swedish, not that he knew Swedish but he'd heard Swedish tourists chattering among themselves. It was all very odd and fishy and quite beyond him. All he could do was report facts. He went on writing.

It was the first time that Alice had heard Alexi lay his feelings for her on the line, openly, without reserve. Even in their most intimate moments he had seemed to withhold something. When he had said, "I love you, little Alice," he had somehow made her feel that it was a formal phrase, something he was expected to say and had therefore said it. She had put it down to a curious amalgam of shyness and a reticence acquired in the course of his work over the years. If he had felt a tinge of sympathy for a suspect he was interrogating he would have thought twice before he displayed it. But now, if only for a few moments, he had discarded all caution. He was speaking loudly, fiercely, striding up and down the room, blue eyes blazing, enjoying the luxury of showing his emotions, freely, and without restraint. Alice burst into tears. It was all so depressingly ironic.

"What are you blubbing for?" Sam offered her a cigarette. "It's nice, what he said, isn't it? Why blub about it?" Alice refused the cigarette.

"I'm just happy, and the happiness won't last."

"I expect things'll turn out all right," Sam spoke without any noticeable conviction.

"It is better I go back, after the dreadful things I have done," Schorin said sullenly. "Where are my naturalization papers? Where is my fine office? In an almshouse for poor people!"

"I can think of easier ways of committing suicide," Sam Letts said. Schorin waved a hand.

"It is better I go back. What will happen is what I deserve."

"If you go, I go." Alice adjusted her glasses. Schorin shook his head.

"Too late, *dusha moya.* Once I asked you to go with me but you said no. You will remember?"

"Things were different then, Alexi."

PC Burns shut his notebook with a snap and stood up. "Well, I'll go now and turn in a report." He opened his notebook again and glanced briefly at what he had written. "I've put you down as Mr. Alexander Hans Larsen, Swedish, temporarily resident at Number Three, the Almshouse, Melford. Three for luck, eh? And you, madam—" He hesitated. "In view of your earlier words I have described you as British, and Common Law wife of the said Alexander Hans Larsen. And you, sir?" He looked at Sam Letts.

"Samuel Letts, journalist. I'm staying at the Blue Boar." PC Burns added the details to the foot of his report.

"We may need you as a witness of what has occurred in this almshouse."

PC Burns put on his helmet, thrust his notebook into his hip pocket and moved to the door. "There's things going on here I don't understand; fishy, I'd say, but it's not for me to probe, sir, that's for others, perhaps. But that's as may be," he added in his slow Melfordshire accent. "Fishy, very fishy, but all I has to do is report a case of breaking and entering and vandalism by a person or persons unknown."

He fixed Schorin with a speculative eye. "I've not mentioned the incident on the stairs, sir, you being a foreigner, and perhaps not as acquainted with our laws as some. No doubt you were over-excited having seen too many of these television thrillers, sir. I've just reported that you suspected that an intruder was upstairs, and called upon him to come down and give himself up. But don't go waving that gun about too much, sir, not if you want to be naturalised. Goodnight gentlemen, goodnight madam."

Sam Letts watched with relief as the door closed behind the officer. An unexpected wind rustled the leaves in the street outside. Suddenly the blue light which had bathed the cathedral disappeared. Work for the Sound-Light pageant had finished for the night. Alice felt cold, and shivered.

Schorin went to the wall cupboard, opened it, and took out a bottle of whisky, some glasses and soda water, which had somehow escaped the attention of the intruders.

"Drink, we might as well drink," he said.

"Alexi, you didn't mean what you said, did you?" Alice spoke timidly.

"What did I say?" he temporised.

Alice sighed. The euphoria aroused by his words of love vanished. His mood had changed, and hers with it. A clammy black hand seemed to be clutching at her heart as she recalled the reason for his outburst.

"About going back," she whispered. Schorin took a gulp of whisky.

"It's not the first time I've thought about it. I'll never be trusted here, I'll never be accepted here. Just another of the walking dead. Over here, it's the running dead. Running from the bloddy KGB. All my life, running. And now there's this thing about you." He finished his whisky and poured out another.

"I'll have another, too," Sam Letts said. Schorin refilled his glass. Alice had not touched hers. Suddenly she got up out of her chair and went to the corner of the room where the telephone stood on a small shelf. Superintendent Brock's police engineers had installed it with the Post Office people. And installed it very firmly. The receiver was hanging down by its flex, resting against the wall.

"Some sod tried to tear it out and then got deflected to something else," Sam said.

"Or left it hanging on purpose, on instructions," said Sugden. "A listening ear." Sam Letts grunted, and belched softly. Alice replaced the receiver, waited a few seconds, lifted it, and when she heard the dialling tone rang Brock's home number, heard him answer, and told him what had happened. When she had done so there was a long silence.

"Are you there?" she finally asked.

"Yes, I was having a word with my wife. She's worried."

"I'm not worried. I'm terrified. For more reasons than one."

"Pack your suitcases, you and Alexi, both of you. I'll come and fetch you. Now. Sugden can stay there. Are there wooden shutters you can close?" She looked round at the windows.

"Yes, there are."

"Close them. I'm coming to fetch you. I want you both to

stay with me. Jane doesn't mind. She used to work in a fishing hotel in Scotland."

"We'll drive over," Alice said.

"No, you won't. And don't go near the car," Brock added firmly, with memories of Northern Ireland. "I'll be over in about ten minutes. Don't let anybody in. I mean it. I'll ring the bell four times—not three times, and not five times. Four times. Got it?"

"All right," Alice said in a resigned tone. If Alexi was going back nothing seemed to matter. She replaced the receiver and looked at Schorin.

"We're moving to Brock's place."

Schorin, unpredictable as ever, stared at her in dismay. He took the automatic from his shoulder and slammed it on the table. "I'm staying, I'm not being run out of my almshouse by a lot of KGB criminals." His voice was indignant, face sulky. Hopeless, quite hopeless, Alice thought, but her grey eyes were alive with renewed hope. Something was stirring at the back of her mind. She forgot whether, in the Aesop tale, the enmeshed lion was grateful to the mouse for helping him to escape, and she did not know if a mouse could challenge a tiger and win, but if Alexi could welcome a challenge, so could she. She knew now that she could influence this difficult man, that he really loved her.

"I'm staying here," Schorin said again. "Here I am and here I stay. The future is the future, I may re-defect or I may not," he added, "but for the moment I am staying here."

"Then you're staying alone. I'm going up to pack." Schorin watched Alice move to the door.

"Bitch, bourgeois bitch," he grumbled, and moved reluctantly after her.

"I'll be off," Sam Letts said, with an unexpected hiccough.

Schorin appeared to be turning something over in his mind. "We'll meet again soon, Sam. For a talk about the book. I'll ring you. Meanwhile I'll run you back to the Blue Boar." Alice swung round from the living-room door.

"No you won't! You won't touch that car. And if you go out you can stay out. I'm locking the door and closing the shutters."

"I can walk, the air will do me good," said Sam Letts.

"I'll walk part of the way with you," Sugden murmured.

"Don't leave us!" Alice pleaded.

"I'll have a look around while I'm about it."

"What for?"

He did not reply because he did not know. He had been silent and thoughtful for some time, wondering how Ducane would react, wondering if he was right to go out to dinner with Brock, or whether he should have stayed to guard the almshouse. Right from the beginning, like Brock, he had been doubtful about the practicality of protecting Schorin, the ill-disciplined defector. He sighed and followed Sam Letts out of the house. He heard Alice call after him.

"Do be careful!"

"Aye, I will, I like to keep healthy."

Meanwhile the tiger meekly followed the mouse out to the staircase. But on the stairs Schorin flared up again.

"Bourgeois bully, typical of your class. I hate all your class. All of you!"

On the landing Alice reached up and put her arms round his neck and kissed him. "No you don't, you love me," she said and kissed him full on the lips.

"Of course I love you, *zadushevny,* I said so this evening."

"For the first time—properly! And in front of witnesses!"

From down below came the sound of the doorbell. It only rang once. Schorin pushed her gently away and walked quickly to the stairs.

"Alexi! Where are you going?"

"I left my cigarettes on the table."

"Don't open the door!"

He stopped on the stairs, and looked up at her. "Of course I won't open the door, darling! Stand there against the light, do you think I'm mad?" She did not reply. She did not think him mad. Just impetuous and reckless among other things. She waited until he came up the stairs again, cigarettes in hand. The doorbell was silent.

While they were packing, Schorin, who had been neatly arranging shirts and pants into his suitcase, stood upright and stared at a cheap framed print on the wall which the intruders had smashed. Alice said: "Never mind that, it was never much of a decoration."

Schorin switched his gaze from the picture and stood looking down at the floor.

"I wasn't thinking about the picture."

"What were you brooding about?"

"Sam Letts."

"What about him? Poor old Sam, he's a soak, he's on his way out."

"Who can trust a drunk? Tell me that. I shall be master of my life or death, that I shall be. I will *not* allow myself to be killed by the bloddy KGB when they wish! If I decide to live or die it shall be my decision and only my decision, it is a matter of——" He stopped ranting, seeking the right word.

Alice left her suitcase and ran across to him. "A matter of what, Alexi?"

"Professionalism. And I do not trust Sam Letts—your former lover," he sneered. "He was a poor choice, *zadushevny.*"

"He was never my lover. He might have been, but he wasn't."

Schorin gave a short imitation of a hard laugh. "Tell that to some bourgeois priest! He may pretend to believe you, but will your capitalist-loving *so-called god?*"

Alice froze up inside. It came easy to her. She had grown accustomed to freezing up when he was in one of his aggressive moods. She found it was the only thing she could do. If she tried to protest he would shout her down. He banged his suitcase shut.

"What are you sulking about?" he asked.

"I'm not sulking. I'm praying to my so-called God to give me patience."

"Good luck to you both. I don't trust Sam Letts, he is a danger. All drunks talk too much."

"Alexi, are you jealous? Jealous of the past? You don't need to be."

Schorin, his packing finished, was sitting on the side of the bed.

"He's still fond of you. I am a trained Intelligence officer, I am able to note these things, I could see it this evening. From the way he looked at you."

"Alexi, he is still fond of me, I think—as a friend. He knows he saved me when I was down. I think he sees himself as a father-figure."

Schorin gave another hard laugh. "What a father, what a figure! Will you listen to something?"

"If I must."

"At the restaurant, when you went out to powder your nose —what a silly bourgeois expression!—he said to me that he thought we ought to get a short article published now, saying that a book was being prepared—to arouse interest, like a piece of bait for fishes."

Alice frowned. "He promised to publish nothing without your agreement."

"Did he promise to stop his heavy boozing and not give a wink, a knowing look, when the name of Alexis Schorin was mentioned by fellow newspaper people? And did you believe that?"

Before she could try to answer, Schorin put a hand on his forehead. A sudden thought had occurred to him.

"Do you think this middle-aged drunk would be heartbroken if I returned to Moscow and left you here alone? Or if, by some means, I hid *you* from the KGB, would he be unhappy if the KGB bastards found where I was and killed me? Or do you think he would return to you and plead like an innocent child for a reward for his past help to you?"

Alice was more shocked than she remembered being for a long time. The implications of his words, the unspoken hint of betrayal by Sam, even allowing for male jealousy, made her feel helpless, and once again she felt herself freeze up inside. She had never before suspected that Alexi might be jealous. But then he had never before expressed his feelings so openly. Jealousy was unreasoning, destructive, and fundamentally incurable.

She fully believed Alexi Schorin was capable of killing for jealousy, and guessed that he had more than once killed for lesser reasons. Sensing that something was seriously wrong, Schorin jumped up from the bed and put an arm round her.

"Little Alice, *dusha moya,*" he murmured in his child-like voice, "do not listen too much to silly things I say, it is only because I love you so much. Maybe I like to torture myself with my silly jealousy. Look," he raised his voice, "if Sam Letts is your friend then he is the friend of Alexis Ivanovich Schorin!"

"You will not do anything silly—hurt him?"

"Why should I? We are all good friends!" Alice dearly wished to believe him. "We will all be happy one day, one way or another!" Again Alice tried to believe him.

From down below came the sound of the front door bell. It rang four times. Alice and Alexi exchanged looks and went downstairs with their suitcases.

Brock was normally unhurried and deliberate in speech and movement. But when Alice unlocked the door and opened it he pushed past her and Schorin like a destroyer in a rough sea, and went into the living-room, nodding and glaring.

"A right old mess," he said in his soft muffled voice. "Have they taken anything?" he asked Alice.

"Not as far as I can see." A thought occurred to her, and she went quickly to the little writing desk which had been provided in case a poor and distressed widow wished to write to some other poor and distressed widow. She pulled open the top drawer and after a while glanced at Schorin.

"The cassette's gone, Alexi," she said nervously, anticipating an outburst. Schorin rarely reacted as expected.

"It was silly of me to put it there," he said sheepishly. "It is my fault. So much is my fault. I have done so many dreadful things."

It was the first time Alice had seen his spirits flag. Her spirits sank with his. But she pulled herself together.

"It was lucky they didn't pull the phone out," she said brightly. "I think they tried, but something must have interrupted them."

"Like second thoughts," murmured Brock, pulling at his big high-bridged nose.

"Or remembering orders?"

"It was hanging down, drooping, like a pop singer who's dropped his microphone," Alice gave a little laugh, determined to keep the conversation cheerful.

"A dangling ear," muttered Schorin and looked questioningly at Brock.

"Not my ear," Brock said, "or Ducane's. Not our ear."

"A KGB ear? They get around, they get around everywhere," Schorin said with reluctant admiration.

"Let's go. They'll know where we're going, if it is one of their ears, but I doubt if they'll try anything more tonight."

"They've tried it," Schorin said. "Before you arrived. Somebody rang the bell." Brock was shepherding Alice and Schorin to the door, pushing them gently but firmly.

"That was PC Burns," he said. "He'd forgotten his pencil. I met him. He told me he rang but you didn't answer."

He pointed to a standard issue police pencil on the table in the middle of the room. But he frowned, because although he had driven past PC Burns on his way to the almshouse he had been too anxious to get there quickly to stop and talk to him. It might have been PC Burns who had rung. On the other hand it might not. It might have been another move in the war of nerves, or it might have been somebody trying to lure Schorin to the door.

"Let's go," Brock said again. He bustled them to the door and into his car.

Later when he and Jane had greeted them with a cup of tea, and settled Alice and Schorin in for the night, Brock lay in bed and grumbled.

"I hate Special Branch work," he said sourly.

"Why, Badger? Work is work is work."

"SB work is nebulous. A crime is a crime, it is either solved or it isn't. If it isn't solved in a reasonable time—okay, it remains on the books but you pass on to other things. But SB work goes on forever, it never ends."

"Oh, go to sleep, Badge."

But he rambled on: "Protection work is the worst, you don't know what you are looking out for. We haven't even got a proper Special Branch in Melford. Force is too small. What have we got? One part-timer, Sergeant Wally Jones, the Welshman—because we're not far from Wales where there's sometimes trouble. Why doesn't the Home Office get a bloody move on with Schorin's papers? How long are we to be lumbered with these types, Jane?"

"You lumbered yourself with them."

"I did not," Brock protested indignantly. "ACC Tomkins lumbered me with them."

"And Ducane lumbered the ACC with them, they're his prize pigeons. That reminds me. Sergeant Wally Jones rang up while you were out. Ducane had rung him, he's coming down tomorrow to see you."

"Oh, good, that'll make my day!"

Jane reached out and turned off the bedside lamp. "Go to sleep," she said again and patted his cheek. "Go to sleep and dream about trout or something."

The following morning Brock wrote briefly in his diary:

An eventful day. Schorin's house broken into and vandalised. A note in Russian left for him, threatening Alice if Schorin does not give himself up to, in effect, the KGB. Sugden said little, which is normal, but Ducane will have a fit because Schorin threatened to re-defect. Luckily he seemed to change his mind when Alice pleaded with him. What a tiresome man he is! So charming and so difficult! I took them both back to my house. Jane was dismayed but agreed it was the only thing to do. The ACC will explode as usual. But it's part of the job, I suppose. ACC Tomkins would have exploded anyway, whatever I had done. Blast all defectors. Would rather cope with the ACC than a defector. But the ACC wants to keep Whitehall sweet with an eye to the future.

CHAPTER 8

Schorin had murder in his heart as he talked with Sam Letts on the little Roman bridge ten miles from Melford. Not that he regarded it as murder. The killing of Sam Letts was a clinical necessity, and a very unfortunate one. He had considered the problem of Sam Letts with the same detachment as when faced with similar problems in his GRU activities. Some dangers cannot be ignored, swept under the carpet, in the hope that they would go away of their own accord.

It was a pity, but Sam Letts knew too much. He knew that the man on his passport and faked birth certificate as Alexander Hans Larsen was in fact Alexis Ivanovich Schorin. Above all, he knew about the plan to emigrate to Australia. That was the most dangerous thing. That was the clue which would delight the KGB and GRU assassin squads. The population of Australia was not as numerous as Britain's. Easier for the KGB to comb with its network.

It was three days after the break-in at the almshouse when Schorin phoned Sam Letts from a call-box and asked him to meet him at noon at the Roman bridge near Melford.

"Don't mention that you are meeting me," he added. "You know why?" Sam had agreed readily enough. Sam was thrilled. The secrecy augured well, it implied mutual trust. Both Alice and Sugden had demurred when Schorin said he was going out for the day, alone. But Schorin was adamant.

"A man needs a few hours to himself," he said firmly.

"Be careful, just be careful," Sugden said in an anxious voice.

"I'll be back in time for evening drinks."

"I hope so," Sugden said. "I do hope so." Alice said nothing.

He slipped out of the house while she was in her bedroom and did not even say goodbye.

It was a beautiful cloudless day, warm but not too hot. He watched a Red Admiral butterfly fluttering aimlessly along the top of the little Roman wall near a spider's web. He had long dismissed from his mind all memory of what he had said about giving himself up to the Embassy. But Sam Letts now referred to it as they stood on the Roman bridge.

"You weren't serious? Brock'll look after you both."

"It was *vranyo*. It's a sort of playful bluffing, an innocent lie. *Vranyo* is leg-pulling, nonsense; it is not like *lozh*. *Lozh* is telling lies with a bad purpose, like Iago, he was full of *lozh* lies. What a beautiful butterfly."

"It's a Red Admiral. You said you were in the navy for a little while, were you a red admiral?" Sam Letts sniggered at his own feeble joke.

Schorin felt his resolve weakening. Was it necessary to kill this drink-sodden creature? Wouldn't his reputation as a drunk make people doubt anything he might say? Even if he said he knew a Russian defector people would only think he was in a drunken boastful mood. Sam Letts patted the right pocket of his jacket.

"Have a swig of vodka?"

"Thank you—yes." Sam Letts pulled a bottle of liquor out of his pocket.

"Well, you can't have it, 'cos it's gin. *Vranyo*," Sam said happily.

Schorin watched him pour some gin into a cup he had taken out of a carrier bag with a packet of cheese sandwiches which he had bought at the Blue Boar. His hand trembled. The half bottle of gin was only one third full.

The Red Admiral, finding nothing nutritious on the top of the wall, had dropped down a foot or two and was fluttering ineffectually nearer to the spider's web. Sam Letts poured out gin into a second cup and handed one to Schorin.

"There's no water, unless you want to climb down and get some out of the river, and that'll be polluted. As our great leader Churchill once said, I have always found the moderate use of alcohol a great comfort. Cheers." He lowered his voice and looked round carefully. "Alexi, old boy, I've been thinking."

Schorin had also been thinking. He had meant what he said when he told Alice he would "play along" with Sam Letts. That was the way the true professional went about such things. Nothing hurried, no unforeseen development. And now? Looking at the burnt out wreck beside him, Schorin's resolve again faltered. It was not that he felt the stirring of pity. It was a wave of something practical. An assessment. Was it worth the effort? The deed, and the disposal of the remains after the deed? The lies and pretences to sad Alice? She would certainly be sad, and perhaps suspicious. More worry and more tension. After the drama and trauma of recent days was it all worth it?

The peace and quiet of life in a faraway warm land were almost to hand. The Home Office surely could not delay his naturalization much longer. He loved the sun and yearned for it. It was the thought of the sun in Australia which attracted him. And the sands and the sea. He had never learned to swim. In the navy, the sailors had said: "If you cannot swim now, better not to learn, better not to know how to swim if you are sunk. Better not to struggle, but to go quickly, Alexis Schorin! Go quickly!" But he would learn to swim in Australia. Every day he would swim and then lie in the sun.

"That bloody silly butterfly is going to flutter straight into that sodding spider's web, Alexi."

"Too bad for it. What've you been thinking, Sam?"

"It's turned back," Sam Letts said, ignoring the question. He sounded glad. Schorin thought that Sam was like the Red Admiral and always would be: fumbling along, hardly knowing where it was going or why, now heedlessly approaching the deadly web, now drifting away.

"I was thinking," Sam Letts said, his mouth full of cheese sandwich, "I was thinking I ought to come with you to Australia. Not to live in the same house, of course, but in the same town."

Schorin said nothing. He saw that down below the Red Admiral, which had been retreating from the web, had had second thoughts, assuming it could think at all, and had done a U-turn. It was facing the web now, poised on a piece of stone, wings fluttering, ready, like Sam Letts, to continue a shaky flight to destruction. He couldn't see the spider, but knew that, like death for Sam Letts, it would arrive at the right moment.

"Alice will be going with you. Two's company, three's none. But I won't be in the way, old boy." Sam Letts belched softly. "Quite fond of old Alice, but I won't be in the way."

"No, you won't be in the way," Schorin agreed.

He watched as the Red Admiral, apparently possessed by a death wish, took to the wing again, circled, and once more approached the web. Sam Letts had watched it, too.

"Bloody silly insect," he said, and finished his neat gin.

"It'll be expensive, Sam. The government's paying for me and Alice, indirectly, but they won't pay for you."

"Can't write the ruddy book with thousands of miles between us, Alexi. Costs money, yes, but you can't pick it up if you don't put it down. That's what I always say, old boy." He peered sternly at Schorin. "That's why we got to have a formal agreement, old boy. Advance of royalties." He noted the puzzled look on Schorin's face.

"Royalties," he explained patiently, "are what an author hopes to get when the book is published and sold. And usually doesn't," he added. "But our book will be a best seller, that's for sure. Worldwide. Can't miss. I'm going to ask ten thousand pounds advance. But I might settle for seven on signature of the agreement and another three when the book is finished. Leave it to me, old boy. Know what?"

"What, Sam?" The Red Admiral butterfly had lurched towards the spider's web, tried to pass it, and had got one wing caught in it.

"I got a date with a publisher next week, old boy. I've told him roughly what it's about. Had to, didn't I?" muttered Sam Letts, thereby signing his own death warrant.

"Did you mention my name?"

"Not directly, but I think he guessed, old boy. Publishers aren't fools, you know. At least not all of them," he added thoughtfully.

"Which day next week?"

"Wednesday afternoon. Why?"

"I might come up with you."

Sam shook his head vigorously.

"Too risky, stay down here old boy, you're valuable property."

"I wouldn't say it is all that safe down here."

"Brock'll look after you."

"I wouldn't say I was a first-class good insurance risk, even in Mr. Brock's house." Or anywhere, he thought.

But almost at once his mood changed. He would make a fight of it. Even if he had only a few years with Alice they were worth struggling for. Life was not worth living, even in Australia, without a challenge. Life, even with Alice, would be like food which was too bland.

On that still day, and in a countryside where there was no movement to excite or disturb, his volatile temperament had been active. First, he had had murder in his heart. Then he had softened. Something like pity for an old and bemused dog had weakened his resolve. Then Sam Letts had revealed his indiscretion with a publisher. So Sam had to go.

He glanced down at the insect. It was still struggling but more feebly, the beat of the wings less frantic. He thought he saw tentacles which might be the spider at the edge of the web, awaiting a time when the meal would be lifeless and easier to eat.

"The publisher might want to see me, if only to be sure that I am still alive, Sam, I might as well come up to London with you." Did it really matter what he said now?

"He'll trust me, old boy. People do trust me, same as I mostly trust other people," Sam burbled on. "I mean, you got to trust people, right? Otherwise all civilised society comes to an end, right?"

"Right," Schorin said mildly. During the GRU training period, when he had been learning English, they had had to read a book about a travelling Chinese story-teller called Kai Lung, one of whose sage remarks had been that there were few problems which could not be solved in one of three ways: suicide, a bag of gold, or pushing your despised opponent over a cliff at dead of night. Suicide was counter-productive, he did not currently have a bag of gold large enough to tempt Sam Letts, and he did not intend to push him over the Roman bridge in broad daylight; but he had never forgotten the words and they were a reassurance. Some opportunity would turn up, perhaps that day, and he would take advantage of it.

The Red Admiral was struggling still more feebly. He, Alexis Ivanovich Schorin, would not have flown so near to the web, not even for a thrill. Sam Letts poured himself out another gin, emptying the half bottle. Then he drooled on.

"Leave the negotiating to me, old boy. I know these monkeys. Just leave it all to me."

"Have you approached anybody else—in the same way?"

Sam Letts hesitated before speaking, noting the hard look in Schorin's blue eyes. "One other. Play them off against each other, eh? We split the net profits, fifty-fifty, right?"

"Sixty-forty, Sam. Forty to you."

"I got to do all the work, Alexi."

"I got all the material."

Schorin pretended to ponder for a moment. What did it matter? He was agreeing terms with a man who was as good as dead. The book would be published, one day, but Sam Letts would not be a co-author. He smiled.

"Okay, Sam. Sixty-forty in your favour."

"I think it's fair, I have given the problem judicious thought."

The last of the gin had affected Sam Letts's speech, and he knew it. He was speaking slowly and carefully, but it took him two attempts to say "judicious." Schorin was watching him, his patience mixed with disdain. The argument had been pointless.

"The book will have you as the author, old boy, my name won't appear, but I'll be the ghost writer, the man who wrote it. You got to be clever to be a good ghost, you got to get inside somebody else's skin," he said solemnly. "But a good ghost can make a lot of lolly, old boy. And this ghost will."

"Fine."

"You trust me, and I trust you. Shake!" Sam Letts put out his hand, and Schorin took it and shook it.

"Ever shaken hands with a ghost before?"

"Not a real ghost, but I've shaken hands with people who became ghosts."

"Ah, that's different."

Schorin had turned away and was looking over the bridge at the butterfly, and Sam Letts did likewise. The Red Admiral had almost freed itself from the web but was still held by one or two strands, and its efforts were weakening. Spiders are mostly nearly blind but the lessening of the tremors of the butterfly's struggles had been transmitted along the strands of the web and told their own story; and the eager diner had emerged fully from its crevice and was now clearly visible, not only to Schorin and Sam Letts but also to the butterfly which had suddenly made a last call on its flagging strength and was fluttering frantically.

"Silly bloody thing," Sam said, enunciating slowly and carefully. "But beautiful, you'll agree about that?" He looked up at Schorin as though genuinely anxious to hear his point of view.

"Yes, it's beautiful but beauty's not enough for survival."

Sam Letts frowned and remained silent for a second or two, as though assessing the validity of the remark. "But beauty is a thing to be preserved."

"It depends on the price, Sam."

"It's loveliness increaseth, it will *never* pass into nothingness," quoted Sam Letts in a maudlin tone.

"Sometimes it does, and must." Sam Letts pushed against the wall and stood upright.

"Are you calling me a liar, Alexi?"

"No, I'm not calling you a liar," said Schorin, to whom drunken belligerence was no new thing. "I'm sure you're right. Shall we load up and go back?"

Sam Letts nodded, his face solemn. "I am glad you are not calling me a liar. Yes, we will go back. All agreed in friendship. But first there is something to do."

Schorin sighed. "What, Sam?"

Sam Letts instantly became aggressive again. "Ah, so you wish to abandon beauty in distress. Beauty is to be rescued. Call me St. George Letts," insisted Sam Letts and pushed past Schorin and peered down at the butterfly. "She is still alive, she knew I would come to rescue her!"

He leaned over the wall and reached down, shouting, "Hold on, my lady, hold on my beautiful lady, St. George is here!"

His right forefinger encircled the strand of the web still holding the butterfly, and he snapped it between his thumb and finger.

A big stone at the top of the wall, which had been roughly replaced by some passer-by, lurched forward beneath the weight of Sam Letts's stomach, wavered for a moment, and fell to the deep water below.

Schorin heard Sam Letts cry, "Christ!" as he followed the big stone down to the water. On the way Sam Letts's head struck a jutting out piece of the wall. A small cloud which had appeared from nowhere, as is the habit of clouds on cloudless days, now obscured the sun. The Red Admiral, mindless of its own narrow escape, fluttered away on some mysterious mission of its own.

Schorin climbed down the bank by the side of the bridge and ran to the water's edge. Sam Letts was lying face down in the water near the bridge. He appeared to be motionless. Schorin, if questioned immediately after the fatal accident, would have maintained that as a non-swimmer there was little he could do except look vainly around for a branch or something similar to throw to Sam Letts; but as Sam seemed unconscious it would probably have made no difference.

There was in fact a short heavy branch which had been blown off a dead elm tree the previous winter, and it lay by the water's edge. He picked it up. The current was edging Sam Letts under the bridge and towards some thick reeds and rushes and a willow tree which grew on the far side of the bridge. Schorin let the piece of wood fall from his hand, and remembered what the Russian sailors had advised, and sighed, and murmured: "Go quickly, Sam Letts, go quickly." Whether it was an order, or whether it was advice, made no difference. Sam Letts had gone to the Great Vintner in the sky, who could turn water into wine, gone to where there were no closing hours.

The swirling stream had carried his body under the bridge. Schorin picked up the piece of wood and climbed up the bank to where the car stood. He felt as yet no pang of conscience. He had seen many worse deaths in labour camps and prisons.

If he felt anything it was relief that a butterfly had performed a dangerous and distasteful task for him. Cirrhosis of the liver would have got the man in the end, but not fast enough. Alive, he was a threat. Dead, he was only a memory of a wreck, once sodden with whisky, now sodden with water.

Schorin walked to the opposite side of the bridge. Sam Letts's body had found a temporary resting place among some rushes. Schorin could just make out his jacket. Motionless, it looked from a distance like a brown farm sack. He hurled that piece of elm wood into a nearby field, and looked over the bridge to where he had found the broken branch. There was nothing else on the bank which could have been thrown to Sam Letts, even if he had been conscious. Or even if he wished to throw it.

Schorin wondered which of his favourite pubs Sam would haunt most, and if he would return to the Royal Court Hotel where the three of them had first met. As he opened the car door he saw that the Red Admiral had returned to the top of the bridge wall and was fluttering ineffectually. He watched it for a few seconds and saw it drop down below the top of the wall as it had before.

He put the empty gin bottle tidily into the carrier bag which the kitchen staff had given Sam Letts. Like many heavy drinkers Sam was not a good eater, and there was still a cheese roll in the carrier bag, and an unopened screw-top bottle of tonic water. Schorin ate the cheese and drank the tonic water and put the tonic bottle in the carrier bag to join the empty gin bottle. He would put the bag in a roadside litter bin on the way back.

He wondered if he should tell Alice about Sam Letts. He had merely said that he was going out into the country for an hour or two to think about his book, and would be back at about six o'clock. He had not told her he was going to meet Sam Letts for several reasons. She would have wished to come along, too. That would mean that she would hear him make arrangements for a further meeting, which he would have arranged if things had not gone his way that day. And she would be uneasy, worried that he might do something to Sam. She was a great worrier. Better to let her remain happily ignorant. It was always better to be firm with women, to tell them what you intend to do, even if you intend to do something else, and leave it at that. No argument. Secretly they preferred it that way. They were like children, who preferred a strict schoolmaster. Such a master gave them a feeling of security. The master might be an old swine but he was strong: strong enough to defend them from unknown dangers.

There was something else he had not told Alice. After running Sam Letts back to the Blue Boar, he had planned to meet Elliet, his chief nestling, his star agent, hand reared, and malleable. What he, Schorin did, was right in Elliet's eyes. If not at first, then in the end. When Schorin adopted his soft wheedling tone Elliet could no more resist it than Alice.

On the day when the news of his defection was spread across the front pages of the newspapers, he had rung Elliet from a phone box and said: "Don't be alarmed. There is more in it than meets the eye. I will explain when we meet again. You are not in danger."

Elliet's sigh of relief was audible even on the phone. "I think I understand," Elliet had said.

"You don't but you will. I will be in touch."

He had not been in touch because there had been no opportunity. Wherever he went he had been conscious of being followed. Once he had caught sight of the ginger headed Sergeant Frost, and sometimes he had seen the Welshman with the thick red lips, Sergeant Wally Jones. He knew it was for his protection, as far as that was possible, but it was irritating, and it had not prevented the break-in at the almshouse.

But now the first heat was off. Ensconced with Alice in the comparative security of Brock's house with police officers patrolling the street outside he felt as safe as he ever would feel until he was out of the country. Like Ducane, ironically, he longed to be bored, to wake up morning after peaceful morning, with no responsibility for other people's lives or actions.

He wished to talk to Elliet for three reasons. First, to reassure him again that whatever other names he might give to Ducane he would never give Elliet's name. Second, he wished to warn Elliet that war between the KGB and GRU had broken out. And careful though he had been to keep Elliet's name a secret, it was possible that the KGB were aware that Elliet was a faithful GRU man. Elliet must be as careful as leading a normal life made possible. He should fit bars to his windows on the grounds that there were so many burglaries, and a bolt and chain to his doors, and go out at night as little as possible.

Third, and most important now Sam was dead, he would try to persuade Elliet to go to Australia. Out would come the old arguments about Brezhnev and his regime, and the conclusion that the best way to serve the world's workers, headed by Soviet Russia, was to do away with the present Russian government. He would make no mention of the loneliness of a defector, nor of the gnawing feeling of guilt which sometimes supervened. Besides, Elliet would not be alone. There would be Alice and himself to encourage him and hold his hand.

Alice had met him once, casually, when Elliet had called unexpectedly at the flat in Ebury Street. Elliet had not stayed long. Just a quick drink and a discussion about arrangements for going to a play at the Royal Court Theatre, and then Elliet had gone, disappearing into the darkness of the street outside like some thin ascetic ghost. A brief enough encounter, but Schorin could tell from the look in Alice's grey and wary eyes that she did not approve of the pale professor.

Aged about forty, thin, balding, withdrawn and inhibited, Elliet was not her type. It did not matter. Schorin took the view that any friend of his must in the end be a friend of Alice. As in the case of himself and Alice, so it had been in the case of Elliet and himself, an attraction of opposites; but where in the case of Alice it was largely physical, in the case of Elliet it was purely intellectual. Older than Schorin, he was steeped in Marxism and Leninism. Indeed it was only when these two subjects were being discussed that he overcame his inhibitions and became voluble.

Trained to detect the slightest deviation from orthodox Communist views, Schorin sometimes believed he spotted traces of Trotskyism in Elliet, and entryism. Once, when he had used the word entryism, Alice had asked what it meant, giving him one of her wide-eyed but cautious looks. And he had replied: "Entry-ism, little Alice, means that you don't knock yourself out hitting against a brick wall—if you can't beat them, join them, and destroy them from the inside. Like mould will destroy a cheese—in the end. First you join 'em, then you affect others, then, when there are enough of you, you come out into the open and smash your enemies. But bourgeois people like you, little Alice, don't know much about entry-ism." Alice, who had in fact learnt a lot about entryism from Ducane, had nodded.

He stood for some time looking down from the Roman bridge at the water below. Once or twice he glanced at the spider's web, but there was no butterfly enmeshed in it, and the spider seemed to have retired into its crevice to wait for a fresh quivering of the web which, like a dinner bell, would signal the arrival of another potential meal. Schorin, gazing down over the wall, was deciding what he should do about the Sam Letts incident. Sam, tiresome in life when drunk or semi-drunk, which meant most of the time, could now be tiresome in death. But he was not a threat.

He decided he would not tell Alice because she would suspect that he had had a hand in Sam's death. Nor would he tell anybody else, including the police. Especially not the police. There were bound to be paragraphs in the press and there was bound to be an inquest and more publicity. He would be called as a material witness. Brock might fix it so that he could get away with giving his new name, but he couldn't prevent a local cameraman taking a picture of him. There had been no time for the facial surgery which Ducane still contemplated arranging. A press photo would blow both his presence in Melford and his cover name of Larsen.

He looked at his Russian wrist-watch, which he would have to discard soon. A pity. It had been with him through some difficult times. But it would have to go. The time was two-thirty. He had arranged to meet Elliet "at the usual place," where he had always met him, twice yearly, when doing his normal round of visits in the West Midlands. Here he would hand over to Elliet what he called his "financial retainer," discreetly enclosed in a brown envelope, and have one of those interminable discussions about the state of the world which they both enjoyed.

Elliet was not a spy in the usual sense of the word. He had two functions. He was a procurer of current non-secret documents such as birth and death certificates, driving licences, passport application forms, forms for radio and television licences, for road vehicle licences, even for dog licences. When a new under-cover agent was being created in Moscow for service in Britain it was essential that his documentation should be impeccably up-to-date. There was nothing illegal or dangerous about passing over such documents, and Elliet was well paid for his services.

His second function, shared with the KGB, was very different. He was a sleeper, a dormouse, installed for the time when an invasion was launched. His rôle then could be vital. He might be supplied with small phials of liquid which could poison whole reservoirs, rendering them useless even for the cattle which normally drank from them. Equally important would be his task of spreading rumours, often false, of bombs in vital factories, of outbreaks of infectious and fatal diseases in certain areas, of transport break-downs, of food-stocks being poisoned. Anything which would cause a disruption of the travel and normal life of the population. His third function, as a trained GRU man, armed with a radio transmitter, was to identify any military, naval or Air Force units he came across.

It is possible that Elliet, with his acute intelligence, may have guessed his possible second and third rôles. If so, he never mentioned them, and Schorin did not. But Schorin knew that, if the crunch came, Elliet would believe that, in the event of a Russian victory, his reward for services rendered could be the opportunity to plunder all the rare books which were now in private libraries.

Schorin imagined him stooping over the faded leatherbound volumes, his small face, usually so dry and parchment-like, alive and pink with excitement. Still looking down at the river below, Schorin realised, as he always had done, that Elliet was mad in a limited way. He was a junkie, and his drug was books.

He would use Elliet, even in Australia. He would keep him on a leash. He got into the car, and drove to a spot about five hundred yards from the Roman bridge, to their usual meeting place. This was in an oak wood in the middle of a field, and a few minutes' walk across-country from the roadway.

Here, opposite one of the bigger oaks in the middle of the wood, the Royal Society for the Protection of Birds had erected a hide. The jays and magpies who had come used the big oak as a stopping off place for wherever they were going and had long since found another and more private resting place.

The hide was in bad condition, its light timber construction, designed to tone in with the surrounding shrubs and bushes, was in a state of disrepair. But the roof, though leaky, still kept off most of the rain; and the wooden bench which ran alongside, facing apertures through which watchers could peer with binoculars, was still in place. The flimsy hut, once a source of harmless pleasure, was now only a meeting place for two far from harmless men.

The meeting was timed for four o'clock. Schorin was fifteen minutes early, Elliet five minutes early. Schorin had watched him through the binoculars he always carried when going on a job. He had seen him park his old Ford Anglia car down the lane, and walk quickly, shoulders stooped, small head down, as he crossed the field to the wood. He had a curious gait, half-running and half-walking. He nodded to Schorin when he entered, and sat down beside Schorin on the long rickety wooden bench.

"I am not being followed," Elliet said.

"I know that."

There was a long pause as though each were trying to find a way of broaching the subject which was on both their minds. Schorin spoke first.

"I suppose you've read the papers, I suppose you were surprised?"

Elliet pulled his long thin nose with the forefinger and thumb of his left hand. His small intelligent eyes peered at Schorin through the thick lenses of his spectacles. He said nothing.

"Well—weren't you?" Schorin was disappointed.

"In a way yes, and in a way no," Elliet replied at length, and looked down at his soft white hands. "To be honest, I have noted in our interesting arguments during the last few years that you had—what shall I say? That you did *not* seem to have the uncritical admiration for Mr. Brezhnev and his colleagues that—well, that I would have expected."

Schorin smiled. "Are you sure?"

"Quite sure. So I was surprised, and yet I wasn't."

Schorin's smile broadened. He looked like a man who had just finished a chess problem. What Elliet had said fitted in with his own sudden recall to Moscow. First, there had been the semi-jocular remark to the Soviet airman, that if he wished for a different life all he had to do was to take to the air and point his 'plane towards Turkey. But that had been a long time ago. Second, there had been the recent brawl in the pub, which hardly merited an immediate recall. But had he made some remark about the Brezhnev regime lately? It was possible, if he had had a few vodkas at some Embassy reception. And had his unwise lack of admiration been overheard, and reported, and added to the other two incidents? It seemed not only possible but almost certain. Maybe there had not even been specific remarks but a general air of non-enthusiasm which had been noted and reported.

Stalin had had people eliminated for even less good reasons. It was thought that if certain circumstances arose, they might not react in a positive way. Stalin might have had his faults but he was a great man. Brezhnev was not a great man, but the KGB was stuffed with Stalinists who sighed for the good old days and despised the GRU. It was that lot who were behind his recall.

It made little difference. The KGB were trying to wipe out the GRU agent network, to monopolise power. He was on their list, and would have been done away with, though in a more discreet way than that used for smaller fry. Had he returned to Russia he would never have left it, not even if he had taken Alice with him as a rich offering. He was glad she had refused. "Come back for consultations," Kuznetsov had reported them as being about to tell him. It sounded complimentary, but he was too old and experienced a hare to be tempted by that vegetable.

A jay which was one of the few which remained faithful to the great oak tree was sitting on a lower branch emitting its harsh cries. He handed the binoculars to Elliet.

"Want to have a look at that bird?"

Elliet shook his head. "I can see it all right. It is pretty."

"It's a robber, an eater of other birds' eggs. Like a KGB industrial spy." Elliet turned his small round head towards Schorin. He fixed him with eyes like black currants.

"Are you sure you're doing the right thing, Alexi?"

"Quite sure. And I think you should come with me to Australia."

"You're joking. Yes, you must be joking!" Elliet's protesting voice suddenly bore a resemblance to the final harsh cry of the jay before it flew off.

"You must be mad, Alexi, the strain of the last few days—"

Schorin interrupted him. "The Melford almshouse where I was staying was broken into. Nothing was stolen except a cassette, you remember the cassette I sent you for your birthday?"

Elliet shrugged. "It is of no importance. Ukrainian and Georgian folk songs."

"I sent you a re-recorded cassette. I kept the original. A souvenir."

"It is of no importance," Elliet said again.

"You have forgotten the last few minutes of it. The joke at the end." Elliet frowned for a moment, then his expression changed, and he laughed.

"Oh, that! You mean where you imitated a sentimental woman and sang a couple of songs?" Elliet produced an imitation: " 'And now two well known songs for Billie Elliet, aged eight, Jill Elliet, aged six, the twins Julie and Jim Elliet, aged ten, all of Aldeburgh Avenue, Worcester, and above all for grandfather George Elliet whose ninetieth birthday it is. Happy birthday, grandpa Elliet, and a happy day to all at Aldeburgh Avenue!' Then you sang *Ghost Riders of the Sky,* and *I Was Born Under A Wandering Star.* Rather badly, if I remember rightly."

Schorin did not smile. Elliet sniggered and said, "I am not a grandfather of twins, as far as I know, and I am not ninety."

"Nor are you likely to be if you stay in England. What is more, you will receive no more money from me, you appreciate that? No more money to be spent on fine books. You are a mercenary agent, primarily, I have always realised that." Elliet considered the remark without rancour.

"Yes," he said at last. "Yes, I am a mercenary. There have been some very fine mercenaries—Ghurkas, French Foreign Legionnaries, and others. Yes, I am a mercenary but in a good cause, the oppressed people of the world. Go your way if you must, I will go mine. I will work for your successor. Give me a name and I will make my own arrangements."

Schorin stroked his hair. "They won't touch you with a barge pole," he said. "The KGB will kill you. You are twice contaminated. You worked for the GRU, with whom they are at war, and you worked for me, a defector. You're almost as dead as I am. But I hope for the best, I take precautions. Come with me, and I will make you tens of thousands of pounds for you to spend on rare books. I am going to write a book myself. You can help me—and make a fortune."

Schorin glanced out of the hide. There were no more birds in sight, neither jays nor magpies nor any other birds. And there was no sound in the wood, as Schorin explained, in the broken down hide, how Elliet could be his trusted friend, and gain riches, and safety from the KGB, in sunny Australia.

"You have everything to gain," he finished, "you might even come back to England if you wished, when the heat has died down. You have nothing to lose."

"Except my life."

"You are my favourite nestling. A nestling is a young bird. You are not young but—"

"I know what a nestling is, Alexi."

"You are special. Hand reared, hand fed. I have told Ducane of others. But I have not told him about you. Not yet." Schorin lingered over the last two words.

The blackmail was obvious and crude. Elliet bowed his head.

"Very well, I will come to Australia with you."

"Splendid!" Schorin said, and meant it. He was astonished at first at the speed with which Elliet had succumbed to the blackmail. Then he was no longer surprised. He knew he had expected it, in his heart. He, Alexis Ivanovich Schorin, was an old pro. And his hand had not lost its cunning. He was gratified that his assessment of Elliet had been right. Elliet was partly mad.

A brilliant expert about books, they were most certainly his drug. At the first hint—and the man's acute brain needed little more than a hint—he had folded up, guessing what the withdrawal symptoms would be like. Who better than a drugged nestling to help him hatch out limitless wealth for himself and his well loved Alice? He was still thinking of the jewels and fur coats he would give Alice when Elliet looked at his watch and said he must be going.

"I have a tutoring session." His tight little mouth stretched itself into a reluctant smile. "One of my few pleasures is the help I can give others with the meagre information I have managed to pick up on my journey through life. It is a great relaxation."

"I am happy for you. I will book air tickets when my naturalization papers arrive. One for you, a little later, for security reasons. We should not travel together. I will post it to you. Ducane will arrange things for us in Australia."

Schorin watched Elliet descend the wooden steps of the hide and cross the field, past the rubbish pit, and along the footpath which had once been flattened by the feet of numerous bird watchers. The worn grass was recovering, the rubbish pit emptied. Tall new grasses grew round the side of it. Nature was repossessing her own. He watched the tall stooping figure of Elliet, with his half-running, half-walking gait, until he reached the road.

Schorin replaced his binoculars in their case and also left the hide. He would be back in time for an evening drink with Alice and Brock and Jane Brock. He had not liked blackmailing Elliet. It savoured too much of his earlier life when he wished to forget, except when it came to writing his book with Elliet. It had not even been delicate blackmail. But he again recalled his theory: a man will do anything when it is a question of survival and a junkie will do anything to get his drug.

Elliet, half-walking, half-loping across the field from the hide, was thinking along similar lines.

CHAPTER 9

When Alexi had left by himself supposedly to brood about his book, Alice had been hurt. She would have liked to have gone with him, but telling him so would have made no difference. She had long ago learned that when his mind was made up, it took a long time for her to change it. If she could.

Jane had set off on her own for some committee meeting of the formidable Melford Women's Institute and would not be back till about six o'clock. She herself intended to return by about five o'clock, to be in Sheldrake Drive when Alexi arrived back after his solitary excursion. She had a hair appointment for two o'clock, and would be finished shortly after three. To fill in time, she decided to stroll along the Mell and look at the swans.

Alexi had been tetchy and irritable for a couple of days, and she was not surprised. The novelty of answering endless questions and being shown an equally endless stream of pictures had worn off. Moreover, in spite of his denials, she guessed that he was jumpy and in constant fear. He still carried his automatic with him wherever he went, despite Brock's remonstrances. His attitude, obstinately repeated, was that he would rather be prosecuted than be slaughtered without a means of defence; and if it were to be taken from him he would simply go up to London and get another one in Soho. Brock had shaken his head with its badger-like streak of hair, but had dropped the subject. Alexi had not repeated his horrific threat to give himself up to the Embassy.

As she walked along the bank in the early afternoon sunshine she stopped to watch two male swans fighting. It was a fascinating but frightening sight. The bigger swan had twined its strong neck round the other one's and was remorselessly bending it down towards the water. When it succeeded it tried to hold the other one's head beneath the water with the intention of drowning it. The smaller one broke the hold and swam away. She wondered if its narrow escape from drowning would give it bad dreams. The thought of disturbed sleep made her remember how Alexi used sometimes to talk in his sleep. Since his defection he had not talked in his sleep. It was as though, having made the jump, the decision had removed one problem from his mind, even though it had been replaced by others.

She knew she would never forget any detail of the awful night before Alexi defected. She sat down on a bench. The two swans were preparing for a second round. The rest of the swans, some ten or more, seemed indifferent to the drama. She wondered if anything amused swans or even interested them, apart from food. It must be nice to be a swan in a peaceful backwater near Melford. Suddenly she stood up and frowned, still mulling over that last night in London. Alexi had, as usual, been annoyed to hear he had talked in his sleep. She had reassured him, saying he had said "nothing much." Anything to pacify him. Now, beside the river Mell, and in a calmness of mind induced by the sunshine and slow moving water, she recalled that after a torrent of Russian words, he had started to hum, "Happy birthday dear grandpa, happy birthday to *you*." And how once before, when he had hummed the childish radio greeting, he had muttered what sounded like "Elli ate." Who was Elli and what had he eaten or "et"? But in the turmoil of that last night in Ebury Street she had made no mental note. Nor did it seem important. Nor, she admitted, staring at the swans, would she have dared to ask him about it.

She had not mentioned the soppy song to Ducane because it seemed trivial and anyway she had been annoyed with Ducane. But now she was friendly with Ducane again. And she recalled how, the night before the break-in at the almshouse, Alexi had played back the cassette, beating time with his hand as the Ukrainian and Georgian songs filled the room. Did a Russian ever cease to love Russia? It was this question that made her frown and try to concentrate the thoughts which were whirling in her head, like black rooks in the sky on a stormy day. For when the folk songs and birthday greetings were over, and the bit too, where Alexi had pretended to be a radio entertainer arranging songs, she had had a sudden inspiration. "Who's *Elliet,* anyway?" she had asked, and her heartbeat had quickened partly with excitement and partly with a premonition of the decision she would soon have to take. Alexi had pretended not to hear.

"Who's Elliet?" she asked again. Schorin smiled indulgently.

"Oh, him—Elliet's just an old professor who used to give me English lessons in London. I've told you once. And I taught him some Russian. Then he moved to near Worcester. We were quite good friends. That's why I sent him a copy recording of the cassette, he can polish up his Russian with the folk songs, and have it as a souvenir. I'll pop over and say goodbye to him before we go abroad—if we ever do," he added angrily, "if they ever procure the bloddy papers." She had nodded and made no comment.

She gazed at the swans. The two male birds were fighting again, but Alice did not care. She had her own problems. Elli*ate* or *et?* Elliet? The one Alexi would not betray? Not so much a nestling as a dormouse. And did the dormouse have a team of smaller rodents? Or had they been swept away by the KGB in the fratricidal war with the GRU? Elliet certainly had not been swept away since Alexi wished to say goodbye to him before they left. But now that the cassette had been stolen would the KGB soon strike at Elliet, putting departmental ambitions before patriotism? Finally, what could Ducane do about Elliet? He had committed no crime yet. She foraged in her mind. Was there not some law against conspiring to commit a crime? But what evidence could there be if Alexi remained silent? His nestling? How could a nestling also be a dormouse? At the back of her mind was the ultimate threat—a delay, perhaps an indefinite delay, in the transformation of Alexi Ivanovich Schorin into Alexander Hans Larsen, British citizen of Anglo-Swedish parentage—if she or Alexi put a foot badly wrong.

For Alice the battle of loyalties was painful. She knew she should tell Ducane what Alexi had cried out in his sleep in Ebury Street. The "strong support" Alexi had muttered about in his sleep clearly referred to a "strong support agent." He may even have mentioned the word "agent." She could not remember, she had been drowsy herself and his rambling words had sounded incoherent and meaningless. Elliet was almost certainly Alexi's favourite agent. The more she thought about it, the more sure she became.

Thin lipped Froggie Ducane always maintained that he did not regard himself as working for British Intelligence, he worked for a bigger community, he swam around protecting the other creatures in the pond, some bigger than himself but more vulnerable. If it came to a crunch, and to war, and sleepers were active with their poisons and their rumour-mongering, Ducane was experienced and clever enough to take to the bushes while the others were being scooped up in nets. And no doubt he would take her with him. But that was not the point and did not solve the problem of divided loyalties.

On the one side was the enchanting, infuriating Alexi, who was exciting because he was so unpredictable, so strong and menacing, so kind and gentle. So full of zest and sometimes so downcast and pessimistic. If he ever learned that she had told Ducane about his nestling he would never forgive her. Not ever. It would be the end, and back to the bed-sitter for which she had so prudently paid rent in advance. On the other side was the tribe in which she had grown up. Her mouth began to tremble again as always when she was upset. She was upset now, because at heart she knew what her decision would be. "They're all the same, these Slav defectors," Ducane had once said. But they weren't all the same. Alexi was unique. She made a last effort to persuade herself that since Ducane could do nothing about Elliet at the moment, there was no point in reporting him. But she knew it was a hopeless struggle.

The two swans were fighting more fiercely than ever, the one still trying to drown the other. Like the KGB and the GRU? The thought served to distract her mind from her misery. She dabbed her nose, and took off her spectacles and wiped the lenses, and walked towards a telephone kiosk ahead.

Ducane sounded irritable when she got through to him. He liked to enjoy his afternoon cup of tea in peace. Unlike other officers who drank their tea out of mugs, Ducane's was brought to him on a tray with a cup and saucer and a dimity teapot, as befitted his rank.

"About our friend," Alice said.

"You mean *your* friend. What about him?"

"I think I know who the nestling is. The one he won't talk about."

There was a long pause. Then she heard a noise between a laugh and a snort. "That's a frog indicating pleasure," said Ducane. "I'll be down in about three hours. Can Jane give me supper?"

"I expect so. I'll scribble his name on a piece of paper, and give it to you when Alexi is not in the room. I don't want him to know that I have told you. Okay?"

"If you say so. It's going to be difficult to take action without—"

"I do say so."

"Okay. Well done," he added grudgingly.

She heard the click as he replaced the receiver. Was it well done? She didn't know. But done it was, for better or worse.

She was trembling as she left the phone box, and decided to walk a little further along the river bank hoping that the peaceful surroundings would calm her. Once again her mind went back to the traumatic morning when she and Alexi had furtively fled from London, and how alarmed she had been when she spotted the black car following, which she could not shake off. And how annoyed she was when it drew up alongside her and Sugden had lowered a window and grinned at her. She wouldn't be taken in like that again. Secretly she was glad of police protection, and grateful to be with Brock and Jane Brock in Sheldrake Drive, with a police officer on duty at both ends, instead of the casual glimpse of any uniformed officer who happened to be on duty in the neighbourhood of the almshouses. That routine had not prevented the break-in.

But now, in the home of the superintendent himself she could sleep with an easy mind. Provided that all went well when Ducane made his flying visit. She hoped that it would. Operation Nestling, as she called it, was launched and she wanted to get it over and done with. She also fervently hoped that Ducane would keep his word and not mention to Alexi that she had tipped him off about Elliet. She thought he would. Despite their earlier row, she still trusted him. All would be well. And what a lovely evening it was.

She heard the cheerful toot-toot of the police car a few yards before it drew alongside her, but when the driver wound down a one-way see-through window she did not see the grinning face of Sugden but a more bony face and the smart checkerboard cap of an officer of the Melford City police.

"Excuse me, madam, are you Mrs. Larsen?"

"Yes. Why?" She made a mental note to ask Ducane to provide her with a means of identification in the name of Alice Larsen. Perhaps a phoney driving licence. A false passport would be better still.

"Superintendent Brock's compliments, madam, and he would like to have a word with you at police headquarters."

"At once?"

"That's right."

"What about?"

"He did not say, madam."

The feeling of intense alarm was still to come, though she sensed its presence. For a few seconds she supposed it might be a message from Ducane to say he had been delayed, and would she get in touch with Brock instead. But almost at once she feared for Alexi.

"I am staying with Mr. Brock, I will be seeing him this evening."

There was a sombre look about the officer's pale face which made her uneasy, and she reminded herself that bad news travelled faster than good news. Was Alexi dead, or had he redefected after all?

"It's urgent, madam. And the Assistant Chief Constable wants to see you at the same time, madam." The pale, bony faced officer spoke of the ACC as though he was referring, if not to God's Deputy, at least to one of his very senior assistants.

"I have to be back at Sheldrake Drive in an hour at the latest," she said and got into the back of the car with a sick heart, and sat down beside a middle aged man in plain clothes.

"Did he mention Mr. Larsen?" she asked, and felt the sick feeling increase while the pain spread over her stomach.

"Or a Mr. Letts?" she asked when the officer did not reply. She was clutching wildly at any straw which could divert her fear for Alexi.

"Did the Super mention the name of Larsen or Letts?" The driver flung the question over his shoulder to the man sitting beside her.

"He didn't mention any names, he just said to bring her in," the man answered indifferently. "He just said it was urgent."

As she had walked along the river bank in the peace of the late afternoon she had been hugging her love for Alexi, and it had produced a warm and hopeful sensation. Now she felt cold and fearful, filled with self-reproach because she had not insisted on going with Alexi.

The car had turned and was gathering speed. They passed the great cathedral, and then the town hall adjacent to the police headquarters. She supposed the driver was making his way to the back of the police station, but when he did not turn off and drive down the side road which led to the rear of police headquarters she said: "You've passed the turning," and then spoke sharply to the man beside her. "Take your hand off my wrist!"

"Just stay quiet," the driver said, and the man in ordinary clothes put a hand over her mouth. She tried to struggle but he was much stronger than she was. The stab of fear and pain which she had felt when she thought Alexi was involved had now sprung out at her again, its sharp point driving out the dull ache of apprehension, replacing it with simple terror.

Like the Red Admiral she had one wing caught in a web but the hopeful spider was not visible. It was sitting a long way off in a building with onion shaped domes, and its web was more widely flung, the strands stronger.

Alice knew she had been trapped. Simply, without a struggle, in broad daylight. The feeling of panic which had swept over her, when she realised it, died down and was replaced by the numbness which is born of despair and is devoid of hope. There was an acceptance of facts, and resignation without bewilderment. There was indeed no cause for bewilderment. It was all so obvious.

Outside Melford, where the road climbed up past Gallows Point the man beside her, small, wiry, with iron grey hair, went so far as to apologise to her when he produced a thin scarf and bound her eyes with it. "Sorry, madam, but it is necessary, you will understand that." The feeling of numbness wore off, the dull ache in her stomach returned. It was not all a bad dream from which she would awaken with Alexi beside her, sleeping peacefully.

She saw and felt nothing except the swaying of a fast moving car, the whine of an engine climbing a hill. The dull ache intensified, mixed with dread and misery, curiously compounded with fleeting exasperation, a knowledge of hurt pride caused by damaged professionalism. Tribal and tradecraft tentacles were still tugging. Ducane on his way soon? Perhaps on his way already, to judge by his eager tone of voice. Soon, Ducane waiting in Sheldrake Drive, but no me, she thought, no slip of paper with the nestling's name scrawled on it, surreptitiously passed to him without Alexi's knowledge. Alexi waiting. Guessing the truth? Apprehensive about what she could reveal? And fearful for her? She scrubbed the last question from her mind. He *must* be fearful for her! He loved her. He had defected for her. The thought of him being sick with worry about her was wretched and brought a lump to her throat. The idea that he might not be worried at all was even worse. She could not seriously entertain it.

But in a mood of self-inflicted masochistic torture she dwelt on it for a brief moment. The tears threatened to trickle down from her eyes. She put up her left hand to rub them away. Her right hand was attached to the grey faced man with what seemed to be a handcuff.

"Don't move the bandage, madam."

"I'm not moving it, just adjusting it." She noted, woman like, that the scarf felt as though it was made of silk.

"Will you light me a cigarette, please? There are some in my handbag." She normally carried them only to offer to others, but she felt the need for one now.

"Mr. Curtis, our friend in front doesn't like smoking in a car, and he doesn't like the smell of British cigarettes. He only likes the foreign ones with long tips, which he gets free."

CHAPTER 10

Detective Constable Browning, reluctantly assigned to temporary Special Branch protection duties by Assistant Chief Constable Tomkins, had had a few beers for lunch and wished to attend to the needs of nature. He postponed the matter for as long as he could. In the end he felt compelled to take action. Dressed in civilian clothes, his orders were to keep Superintendent Brock's house under observation and also discreetly to follow Alice if she left it to go into the town. It was the prospect of this which worried him. A lady could take a long time when shopping.

He left his chosen observation post, and turned down a footpath towards some trees and shrubs. But they did not provide adequate cover. He remembered charging some youth years previously, the charge being, "that he did micturate in a public place." He wandered on a little further until he found a good spot. Then, feeling easier in mind and body, he hastened back to his post. During his absence Alice had left for her hair appointment and was no longer in sight.

At four o'clock the Welshman, Sergeant Wally Jones, drew up on his rounds and lowered the driving window of his car, soft brown eyes friendly, thick red lips parted in a smile.

"All quiet with you, is it?" he asked cheerfully.

"All quiet, sergeant."

Alice was quiet, too, in the car descending the other side of Gate Hill, destination unknown. One reason for her being quiet was the second silk scarf which Grey Face, apparently called Alan, had produced, seemingly as an afterthought, and tied round her mouth. But he did not tie it very tightly. It was not uncomfortable. Again he apologised, since it was his habit always to be polite to anybody who might not have long to live. He had said so more than once to his KGB Controller.

Alexis Ivanovich Schorin returned to Brock's house in Sheldrake Drive shortly before six o'clock. He was in one of his exuberant moods, which would have delighted Alice, since it portended a happy evening, likely to be free of sulkiness and filled with carefree amusement. An evening which made it worthwhile putting up with other evenings of bad temper and tantrums.

Everything was going his way. The unfortunate Sam Letts was no longer a menace. Elliet had agreed to come to Australia and help him with his book. There was a full bottle of vodka in the cupboard. They would all have a merry booze-up that evening, except Jane, who didn't drink much. He was still cosseting the feeling that everything was going his way as he opened the front door and let himself in. He even had a passing thought that perhaps the KGB would not succeed in killing him if he could soon make a getaway to Australia. It would be a good evening. He felt sure of it, and wondered if one bottle of vodka was enough. He guessed that Brock might still be at his office, and knew that Jane's committee meeting was open ended as far as time was concerned. But when he called Alice's name he expected a reply and was disappointed that she was not at home to welcome him. Perhaps she was upstairs and had not heard him. He banged the door shut and called her name again. But there was no reply. Perhaps she was lying down on her bed upstairs asleep. She sometimes took a late afternoon nap in preparation for the evening. He called her name a third time. It was then he felt the weight of true silence, a void filled with a heaviness that cannot be measured.

He ran upstairs and gazed at the empty bedroom and checked the bathroom in case she might have fainted; or dozed off in her bath. He stood, uneasy, at the top of the stairs. Outside even the noises of the town seemed to have been hushed, as though the whole of Melford were listening with him, waiting with bated breath for something to happen. If a mouse had moved he might have heard it. But the only noise he heard was the almost imperceptible whisper of the blood making its way through his ear drums.

Then normality returned. A distant car hooted three times, a heavy lorry rumbled. A faulty burglar alarm raised its ugly jarring voice and went on screaming for attention, a car approached from where Sheldrake Drive joined the major road, and came nearer and stopped outside the house. Schorin went downstairs as Brock, back unusually early from his office, let himself in.

"Nobody's in," Schorin said, as Brock put his gloves down on the table near the door.

"Well, we're in," Brock said lightheartedly. "Let's have a drink, then I'll go out and nip off the tops of the second sowing of broad beans, they're getting black fly as usual."

"Nobody's in," Schorin said again.

Brock shrugged. Like Sergeant Jones, he had checked with Browning and received a similar answer. If the women had left, Browning should by rights have gone, too, to keep Alice, at least, under discreet protective observation. There was probably a simple explanation. Despite the trouble at the almshouse, he was still of the firm opinion that nothing dramatic would happen in Melford.

"Jane said she didn't know when she would be back for certain. They're a gabby lot, that committee," Brock said.

Sensitive to atmosphere, he caught more than a whiff of Schorin's uneasiness. And some of it affected him. Apprehension is contagious and hard to diagnose at first. No point in letting Schorin know that he was puzzled. Schorin was jumpy. Understandably.

"What about that drink?" Brock moved towards the drinks cupboard.

"What about Alice? What about her?"

Brock turned round. "What about her?"

"She only went out to have her hair done—in the early afternoon. She ought to have been back hours ago."

"Maybe she went on to do some shopping."

"Shops have been shut an hour ago," Schorin muttered.

"Perhaps she met somebody she knew—the Assistant Chief Constable, or somebody, and is having a drink with him. Or Sam Letts, that's quite likely."

Schorin shook his head. That was one person she had not

met. "She would have telephoned by now. It's unlike her," he said evenly.

"Sometimes it's difficult to phone when you want to. Some chatterbox in the phone box. Somebody else waiting. Or box vandalised. Machine out of order."

Schorin remained quiet, frowning.

"I should think that's the answer," Brock went on, turning again to the drinks cupboard. "I should think she bumped into Sam Letts—or Sam Letts bumped into her, that's more likely," Brock said and laughed.

Schorin felt indignation beginning to bubble inside himself. It was all very well for this badger haired superintendent to make up stories about what might or might not have happened. He was in his homeland.

He had a career, a house, a wife. Like Alice, Schorin came up against a hard iceberg of reality. What had he got? No country, no home. No proper job. Promises, tattered and unfulfilled. And the renewed certainty that somebody would kill him in the end. A bitter thought. What had he got—except Alice? A wave of loneliness swept over him

"I bet she's having a drink with Sam Letts," insisted Brock.

Schorin took the vodka and nodded his thanks. Schorin wished the Superintendent would not go on and on so much about Sam Letts. He was feverishly trying to make up his mind about whether to tell Brock the truth or not. He was tempted to say: "I hope she is *not* having a drink with Sam Letts. Sam Letts has drunk more water this afternoon than he has drunk for a long time. Sam Letts is dead. Drowned. He's lying among the reeds near the Roman bridge. You can just see a bit of his jacket. Brown. Rather like the one I'm wearing. I saw him fall as he leaned over the bridge to help a butterfly caught in a web. There was nothing I could do, I can't swim. The river runs deep and fast under the bridge. He'd had a few drinks. He hit his head. He boozed a bit. But a nice chap."

The story was plausible. And true, more or less. Brock would say he could fix things. But could he? Could Ducane, come to that? In Russia they could. KGB and GRU both could. But here? Bloody British formalities. He could hear

Brock and Ducane saying, *"Oh yes, we'll fix things, don't worry."*

"Sam Letts may have taken her out to a country pub for a drink. Had a puncture. Engine trouble. Anything."

Schorin said nothing. Training and instinct kept him silent. Never say anything unless you have to. A man will do anything to survive. Saying nothing was the easiest cop-out of them all. There were footsteps in the hall and they both swung round.

"That's probably her now," Brock said cheerfully.

"Got held up by arrangements for the Expiation Day thing," Jane said, coming into the room. "Sorry. What time do you want supper?" She looked at them and smiled. "You look like the fag-end of a funeral wake."

"Alice is not in," Brock said. "Alexi is worried. I told him she's probably having a noggin with Sam Letts."

Schorin moved quietly over to the drinks cupboard and poured himself out another vodka, forgetting to ask Jane what she wanted. Brock took his place by the cupboard.

"Gin and tonic, Jane?" She nodded.

"Please. I need one after that meeting."

He brought the drink over to her. Their eyes met as she took the glass. Each knew that the expressionless blank look they exchanged was deliberate. He nodded towards Schorin.

"I told him Alice had probably met Sam Letts and was having a quick one with him."

Jane said: "I expect you're right, Badger. What do you want for supper? A quick liver and bacon with a fried egg and a tomato?"

"Fine," Brock said.

"I don't want anything," Schorin said.

"I'll cook you something all the same," Jane said. "And some for Alice, and put yours and hers in the oven to keep warm till she gets back."

"If she gets back." Schorin swallowed his second vodka at a gulp.

"I'll ring the Blue Boar," Jane said briskly. "They might know something."

"Four-seven-seven is the number," Brock murmured. They

waited while she dialled it and spoke, and saw her put down the receiver.

"Sam Letts went out this morning with a picnic lunch. He didn't say when he would be back. It was a picnic lunch for two." Brock raised his eyebrows, but Jane shook her head.

"Alice was *here* for lunch, Badge."

While Schorin had been talking to Elliet in the wood near the old Roman bridge, Alice was leaning against the back of the rear seat of the car, knowing she had been kidnapped. The thudding of her heart slowed down, and the initial shock died and was replaced by other feelings. Bewilderment again gave way to mortification and anger. Her anger was not directed against her captors; her anger was directed against herself. It had all been so simple. She had a two-second flashback and heard her mother saying, "Never accept lifts from strange men, dear." She would be scathing if she were alive. So would Ducane, so would Sugden. And she imagined Alexi pacing up and down, looking at his wrist-watch, shaking his head, also angry or worried or both.

"I'm supposed to be back in time for drinks before dinner," she murmured. The stupidity of the remark appalled her as soon as the words were out of her mouth.

"Afraid you're going to be late, miss," said her companion on the back seat. "She's going to be late, sir, isn't she?" he added with a laugh, speaking loudly so that the driver could hear.

"Unless Alexis Ivanovich Schorin perhaps comes to fetch her," said the driver, accelerating to pass a slow moving farm tractor.

The dull ache in her stomach which was never far away in moments of stress suddenly plunged back, and she felt sick.

She would have given her life for Alexi, not willingly, because in a way it would be counter-productive, but unhesitatingly if circumstances required it. She thought Alexi would do the same for her. It might depend on his mood. But whatever his mood he would not fall into a trap as she had done. She could hear him saying, "Bloddy silly," mispronouncing the adjective as usual, speaking as though he had a mouthful of liquid he had been unable to swallow, or had a large round pebble in his mouth. If Alexi walked into a trap it would be with his blue eyes open knowing what he was doing, going down fighting. And perhaps taking her with him. If he went, she went. It would be better that way. He was all she had to love, and she knew she had to have somebody to love.

After what seemed like twenty minutes she felt the car slow down and turn left. The driver, who appeared to be called Curtis, pointed something out to his companion. His voice was gravelly.

"That's supposed to be a Roman bridge, Alan, that's the local story. They have found a dead body in the reeds near it."

"Whose?" asked the man called Alan, voice polite but indifferent. "Anybody we know?"

"I did. Slightly. Had a few drinks with him in the Blue Boar bar. Journalist. Drank a lot."

The car slowed down again, then seemed to turn to the right. There was the sound of tyres moving on gritty ground. She guessed it might be the drive-in leading to a house.

"He knew our traitor. Didn't say much about where he is, but enough for me. He said a charity house was an odd place to lodge an important man in. He meant an almshouse, of course. The rest was easy." They were chattering away openly. As if she wasn't there. Or if she was listening, then it didn't matter, because she would not be there much longer. Or anywhere much longer. The ache in her stomach had intensified when she had heard Curtis the driver mention a hard drinking journalist staying at the Blue Boar. What had happened to Sam? Alexi had promised not to hurt him. Was it Sam? She wanted to ask more but the gag prevented her from doing so.

Her guess was that they were going to kill her—whether Alexi came to fetch her or not. If he came, the only thing he would find would be her dead body, if that. Then they would kidnap Alexi or, more likely, get him to return voluntarily to Russia with the false promise that he would find her there safe and sound. She did not formulate the sentence in her mind— "They are going to kill me"—but she felt sure of it. She did not want to die. How would they do it?

Her thoughts became confused. She had read that it was usually done with a shot in the back of the neck as you walked along a prison corridor. The short stroll along the river Mell had been pleasant. You did not see the gun they used. It had been a beautiful afternoon. They did it humanely. The sun had been warm, most of the lazy looking swans peaceful. But was it ever humane to kill a healthy person? It had been hot in the phone box when she had rung Ducane. Perhaps she should have mentioned Elliet's name? But Ducane would not have approved. An open line. Not even the doubtful security of a scrambler. Alexi would not have approved either. Not professional. Elliet was Alexi's favourite nestling. What had happened to Sam? Cool, it had been cool by the river, compared with the heat in the phone box.

"Never accept a lift from a strange man," over and over again she had heard it. Repetitious, till in the end the words made no impression. If mother hadn't been so repetitious she would have taken more notice. But a man in Melford police uniform was hardly a strange man. Yet it was mother's fault. Repetition had dulled the sense of the words. Mother loved her, yes, but repetition became boring, dulled the effect. Mother's warning would have killed her. Would it hurt? Perhaps not unless she struggled and made them aim badly. The sun was beginning to set, the sky cloudless and friendly, sad to leave it all. But better with Alexi, they might kill him, too, when he came to fetch her, if he did. Perhaps not in the neck. These two were English by the sound of them.

The uniformed man had got out of the car. Minutes passed. He seemed to be having trouble opening the door of a house. She could not see the house, only a part of it. The man calling himself Alan had undone the scarf over her face, and freed her hands.

"Don't try anything silly, will you, miss? It makes things easier, if you take it easy yourself, madam. Right?" She wished he would make up his mind whether to call her miss or madam. But she nodded. "Put on a good show if it comes to it," Ducane had said years and years ago when she never thought it would come to it. In his office. A distant lion had roared agreement.

Dear old Froggie, a good guy provided you were on his side, so was stocky Sugden with his thick body, and thick ankles and wrists and thick Yorkshire accent, all concealing a paper-thin skin and a guilt complex about the girl he had jilted. And the cop who looked like a badger, and his wife with flaxen hair and the Scottish lilt in her voice. All good guys, doing their best.

"Take it easy, miss," the man Alan said again. Kindly, almost fatherly. She could hardly believe it was happening. Automatically she opened her handbag and took out her old powder compact which Alexi had given her on a day when they had visited the Lanes in Brighton. She dabbed at her nose and covered the remains of some tear stains, and the effort needed to put on a good show steadied her. What the heck? We all had to go some time. She would rather have gone with Alexi, his arm supporting her, but you can't have everything.

She heard the sound of footsteps crunching on the gravel and the passenger door by her side was opened for her by Curtis in his phoney police uniform. He helped her out without speaking, and put a hand on her forearm and led her into the house.

From the brief glimpse she had before she entered it she was not sure whether it was a small, working farm-house or a well built, sturdy cottage visited at weekends by town dwellers. The walls were thick, the stonework mellow and honey coloured. What had probably been a front lawn had been dug up and converted into a wide space for cars. But there was a flower bed with hollyhocks and sunflowers, and a few begonias; and a good many weeds which seemed to suggest that the owners had not been there recently.

Curtis led the way, the man in plain clothes called Alan followed behind her. A steep staircase led from the narrow front hall past a living-room. No overcoats hung in the hall. As she passed the living-room she saw a chintz covered settee and armchairs, a television set, and vases which had no flowers in them. At the top of the stairs Curtis stood aside to allow her to enter a plainly furnished bedroom with two single beds. She looked at him, a question in her light grey eyes. "You can lie down and have a rest for a few minutes," he said. "I've got a few things to fix up with Alan here. I'll call you when I'm ready."

"I don't want to lie down."

She was wary, without knowing exactly what to be wary of, sensing mortal peril but not knowing how it would present itself. Despairing, too, the will to put on a brave front ebbing away.

It was all right for Ducane, gazing safely over Regents Park, to issue airy suggestions about putting on a good show. And Sam? Poor Sam. Nearing breaking point, on the edge of panic and undignified pleading, it occurred to her that if they were using her as a decoy to catch or kill Alexi she still had some minutes to enjoy the setting sun. And the swallows, coming and going repeatedly to nests in the eves. Curtis had seemed to be of medium build when he sat at the driving wheel. Standing up, he proved to be of above normal height. A tall, loose limbed man with long arms and red hands which protruded out of his sleeves; and dark hair, and a bony face-structure like that of the man called Alan, and eyes which were grey, like hers, but of a deeper hue.

"What do you want?" she asked, for the fourth time since they had left Melford, and tried to make it sound a genuine question.

"A telephone call. From you to Alexis Ivanovich Schorin. Asking him to come and fetch you at the Roman bridge. Alone. We shall make sure of that. We shall not be there ourselves. But if he comes alone somebody else will meet him and lead him to where we shall be."

"Who will meet him? Elliet?"

Curtis shrugged. "Does that matter to you—now?"

"And if I refuse, or if he won't come to fetch me?"

"We will try again, first sending him a lock of your hair to show we mean business."

Curtis had pink lips which always looked moist. He passed his tongue over them and they glistened. "Or we might send a finger," he added, "perhaps the one with the ring on it."

"Mr. Curtis has anaesthetics, madam," said the kind voiced Alan. "It won't hurt, miss. Might be a bit sore when the anaesthetic wears off, but bearable, quite bearable, miss."

Her mother had used a similar tone when Alice had gone to

the dentist to have a childish milk-tooth extracted. What did it matter? She would not need anaesthetics if she were dead.

"I'll speak to him," Alice said in a voice hardly above a whisper. "And if he agrees to come and you capture him, what then?"

Curtis shrugged. "We'll have to think."

"I won't be much more use to you, will I?"

"Not much." Curtis avoided meeting her eye.

She knew neither of them could be Elliet. These were KGB hunters, Alexi was GRU. So, obviously, was Elliet, as she would have told Ducane had she had the chance. Too late now. Too late for evening drinks and supper, everything was too late. She had met Alexi too late. The chance of happiness had arrived too late. One had done one's best. Nothing now but to put on a good show for the final exit, or try to. She would speak to Alexi. For the last time. Shriek at him. Something short and vital, perhaps six words before she heard the crash of the shot in the back of the neck. Alexi would have died for her and she could do the same for him: "Stay away! I love you, darling!" Then sleep and the great adventure. But a pity to go on a beautiful evening and without a kiss.

Having made up her mind she suddenly felt calm. Decisions, even small ones, worried her, yet this one presented no problem at all. There was no choice and thus no mental struggle.

Curtis with his high cheeked face-bones again licked his already glistening lips, though he was no sadist. Far from it.

He was a good husband to the Russian wife he said he had met on an Intourist trip to Moscow and Leningrad, and whom he saw so seldom. And he would be a good father to his half-Russian children when the Party ruled the world, directly or by proxy, and when he would be summoned to join the elitist heroes like Philby and Blake.

He had told her about his wife and children just before they arrived at the house. He had related the story to try to interest her and keep her quiet so that she would not suddenly make a fuss which might have attracted attention. Meanwhile orders were orders, especially when they came coded and direct from Moscow, where the wise ones directed his every move—who he should meet, when, where, and what he should do.

Bullies are not all cowards and hatchet men are not all automatons blindly carrying out orders. Curtis was obedient and ruthless, but not a fool. He suspected what had gone on in Alice's mind.

"Don't try to do anything stupid," he warned, and took his revolver from its shoulder holster, and ostentatiously examined it to make sure it was loaded. Not that it would make any difference, he thought, if she tried to do what he suspected. He had shown her the gun, but she was wrong if she believed he would use it while she was on the phone. If the traitor Schorin heard the shot he would assume she was dead and would not come. She was only of use while Schorin thought she was alive. What had to be done would be done—after the phone call, whether Schorin agreed to come to a rendezvous or not. It was a one-shot ploy. Literally. All the talk about locks of hair and severed fingers was nonsense. A psychological build up. Unrehearsed inspiration, and comrade Alan had played up well. She might play ball more readily, create no distressing scene, if she saw a vestige of hope.

He looked at her. Small and slim. Her lips were trembling. The light grey eyes behind the glasses held a hopeless expression. A lamb being led to the slaughter and knowing it. He dried his moist lips with a sleeve of his jacket, and still stood looking at her. Pity was stirring uncomfortably, clouding his mind. Hating what Moscow Centre said he had to do.

He had a quick memory flash of the spade in the boot of the car and the big wooden box. Empty now, except in the mind's eye, but furnished by imagination, before the event, with a folded figure, lying awkwardly on her side, eyes shut, a hand clutching her broken big lensed spectacles.

Curtis did not shudder. Shuddering was for later. But he was not only depressed, he was puzzled. Centre's assessment had been: *Looks soft and pliant, but is tough. She will never break. Schorin may come voluntarily. Not her. Getting her out of the country alive too difficult and risky. She must go. Leave details to you.*

But she had indeed broken. She was willing to co-operate, to telephone the traitor Schorin. So why kill her? He toyed with the idea of contacting the Centre via the radio in the car which was only to be used for dire emergencies. But he put the thought aside. The wise men must have their reasons. They always had, they were always right. What had to be had to be. He sighed.

"I want to go to the bathroom," Alice said. "I want to wash, and do my hair, and powder my nose."

Curtis nodded. Fear sometimes affected people that way.

"Join us downstairs when you are ready."

"Don't try anything foolish, miss," the gentle voiced Alan said anxiously.

"Then I will get Alexis Schorin on the line for you. I suppose he is still staying with Superintendent Brock?" Curtis asked.

She did not answer, but went out of the bedroom and along the passage till she found the bathroom. She heard Curtis and Alan go downstairs. When she had made up her face she looked at herself in the mirror and was reasonably satisfied. Perhaps she was a little pale? She reopened her handbag and added a touch more rouge to her cheeks. Nothing more to be done by way of putting up a good show.

She began to make her way downstairs, very slowly because her legs felt weak. Curtis must have heard her, for she noted the ping of the telephone bell, and Curtis's voice asking to speak to Alexi. Then another ping as the receiver was replaced. Curtis looked round as she went into the drawing-room.

"Somebody told me to go to hell," he said. "It was not Alexis Schorin. I'll ring again, and you can speak to him if he answers, and ask to speak to him if he doesn't."

He lifted the receiver to try again, and then replaced it, because a car drew up outside. Curtis and Alan went out to it. Looking out of the window Alice saw a short stocky man and a woman get out of the car. Curtis and Alan went up to them. They seemed to be arguing. After a while, Curtis came back while Alan went over to the car and unlocked it. Curtis came in and stood in the doorway of the drawing-room. His face was flushed and angry.

"There has been some mistake," he said shortly. "We must rearrange things. The owners of the house have come back a day earlier than expected. We must go. Come." She shook her head.

"You go. I'm staying here." Her heart was thudding even faster than when she was descending the stairs. Curtis glared at her. All pity gone.

"It will make no difference. Not in the long run. We shall get Schorin. And you. There is no complete protection. I doubt if you will even get back to Melford, let alone Australia," he added viciously.

He hesitated, then, as though choosing his words with care, he said softly, "Perhaps something could be arranged. Not for Schorin, but for you. So come. Take it easy, I will do my best for you," he added.

"It's a bit late for that. No." She stared at him defiantly. Centre was right, Curtis thought, unable to hear her thumping heart, she's an iron butterfly, soft outside, but inside as tough as an old boot, Centre was always right. And Centre would be furious. They didn't like plans to go wrong.

"Come, and I will do my best for you," he said again.

"No."

"You are making a mistake. Next time—" He hesitated.

"Next time what?" she whispered.

"Next time I won't make it easy for you."

His dark grey eyes became darker, and did not suit his red bony face. She heard the gentle voiced Alan talking to the new arrivals outside. Curtis strode across the room to the telephone, and tugged the flex from the wall. Then he walked past her and out of the house without saying another word to her. She heard a car door slam and the noise as they drove off. Reaction set in. She could have wept with relief.

The short stocky man came into the house with a woman Alice assumed to be his wife. From outside came the sound of car gears being changed. First to second, second to third, and third to top. Then silence.

The man came into the living-room, and put down the two suitcases he was carrying. His wife was casting a quick look round the room.

"I'm so glad to see you, you've saved my life," Alice said in a tremulous voice. "Yes, you have, who are you, are you the owners of this house?"

"My name is Fred Bradshaw, and that's my wife, Madge, and I do own the house, and who are you, madam?"

"Alice Robins." She sat down on the window seat, glad to take the weight off her shaky legs. "They were going to kill me," she added. "If you hadn't arrived—"

"Why?" Bradshaw scratched his bald head, and looked at her suspiciously. "Those were police officers. They don't kill folk."

"They weren't police officers."

"They said they were. Why didn't you go with them."

"Because they wanted to kill me, like I said."

"Ah." Bradshaw exchanged a glance with his wife. Like her husband she was short and round bodied, with dark brown hair streaked with grey. She was looking at Alice with black beady eyes exuding disbelief.

"I'll nip upstairs and see if anything's missing," she said abruptly and went out of the room.

"They *were* police officers," Bradshaw insisted. He had put down the suitcases, and was staring at them rather than at Alice. Having flatly contradicted her he seemed unwilling to meet her eye. "One was in uniform, and one wasn't, and they were in a police car," he added.

"I know, they used it to kidnap me."

"They did?"

"Yes, they did, but it wasn't a police car."

"But you just agreed it *was* a police car, Miss Robins."

"It looked like one, but it had one-way-see-through windows. You could see out of the car if you were in it, but you couldn't see inside it if you weren't in it, if you understand what I mean?"

She was speaking rapidly, words jumbled and confused as she pleaded to be understood.

"Why did you get into it, Miss Robins?"

"They said somebody wanted to see me. Another police officer, though actually he isn't a police officer. Not really."

Bradshaw could hear his wife moving from room to room

upstairs, and wished she would hurry and come down. He was remembering what the man in plain clothes had said when they arrived. "Mentally disturbed, poor lady. Said she lived here. We don't think she'll come with us, sir. We'll send for an ambulance. Don't want to take her by force. Poor lady." That's what the quiet man had said.

Frederick Bradshaw stroked his chin thoughtfully. He heard his wife's footsteps on the stairs. When she came into the room she said: "Everything's in order upstairs, Fred. In fact, it doesn't look as if the place has been used. Bit dusty, beds not slept in, no clothes in the cupboards, and they took nothing with them."

"Councillor Shingler fixed it, said the police might want it for a week to put up visitors from other Forces for the Expiation Day pageant, as I told you."

Alice was staring out of the window. Bradshaw looked at his wife, his brown eyes dull and bovine, and surreptitiously tapped his forehead and pointed silently at Alice. His wife nodded, her eyes alert and scared.

"The lady says people kidnapped her," murmured Fred Bradshaw. Alice swung round, raised both arms and then let them fall in a gesture of hopelessness.

"They did! And they tied me up with scarves and things, so that I couldn't shout or see."

"Dear me, what a strange thing to happen," said Madge Bradshaw in a soothing voice. "Where did it happen, dear?"

"In the middle of Melford—well, by the river."

"Good gracious! Why did you get into the car, dear?"

"They said they were taking her to see a police officer who wanted to talk to her, but he wasn't a police officer," explained Bradshaw.

"It's a long story," interrupted Alice.

"She says they were going to kill her," Fred Bradshaw winked at his wife.

"Why would they want to kill you, dear?" Madge Bradshaw asked.

"It's a long story," muttered Alice again.

"Fancy that sort of thing happening in Melford," Madge

Bradshaw said, trying to humour her. "Never mind, dear. We live in stirring times, I always say to Fred, so unlike the days of dear Queen Mary. You're all right now."

"They've gone to fetch some friends of hers with whom she's staying," Fred Bradshaw said, with a cheerfulness he did not feel, carefully omitting any mention of an ambulance. "What about a nice cup of tea, Madge? They'll be back soon, they said. Just time for us all to have a nice cuppa."

"I won't go with them or their friends," Alice said firmly. "They will kill me."

"But they didn't kill you when you were staying with them, dear," Madge Bradshaw said. "Why should they want to kill you now, dear?"

"They're not bringing back the friends I was staying with."

"They're just coming back to show your friends the way, whoever they are," Fred Bradshaw said to break the silence.

Alice started to sniff. "I've left my handbag upstairs."

"It's in the bathroom, dear," called Madge Bradshaw as Alice walked hastily out of the room and ran up the stairs.

Fred Bradshaw looked at his wife and shook his head. "We've got a ripe nut here," he whispered.

"Don't leave me alone with her, that's all, Fred, she might get violent."

"She don't look a violent type to me."

"They're the worst. All sweetness and light outside, and then suddenly, bang, and they've hit you over the head with a hammer, and cut your throat. I'll go and put the kettle on."

She moved to the door but stopped as she heard Alice coming down the stairs.

"It'll probably be at least another hour before the police get back," Fred Bradshaw said. "Keep her talking, dear."

Alice swept into the room with her handbag, her mind made up. She couldn't tell them everything, but as a last resort she would tell them something, and to hell with the Official Secrets Acts. Madge Bradshaw gave her an opening.

"Why would police officers want to kill you, dear?"

"Because they're not police officers, they're agents working for the Russians in disguise."

"Ah," Bradshaw glanced again at his wife.

"And I'm not going with them or any friends they've gone to fetch."

Madge Bradshaw's eyes blinked. "Why do they want to kill you, dear?"

"Because I know too much, that's why."

"Ah," said Bradshaw darkly, with yet another glance at his wife.

"And I know a Russian Secret Service defector." Her voice died away as she noted the disbelieving expression on their faces.

"Tell you what!" said Bradshaw, "when they come back I'll go with you, see that you're okay, right?"

"No, you won't, Fred Bradshaw!" Madge spoke sharply. "You're staying with me! It's lonely here."

"I'm not going with them!" Alice sounded obstinate.

Fred Bradshaw cleared his throat. "It's a bit difficult. I mean, you'll have to go sometime, if you see what I mean? We've got our son and his wife arriving and—" Madge helped him out with an inspiration of her own.

"Do you live in Melford, dear?" Alice nodded.

"Why don't you telephone these friends you know, ask them to fetch you, make some excuse or other, not feeling well or something?"

"How?" asked Alice. "They tore the flex out of the wall." She pointed at the flex hanging down from the instrument. "The man in the phoney uniform did it before he left."

The Bradshaws glanced at the damaged phone, then back at her. Neither of them said anything. Bradshaw's dull eyes looked startled, Madge's were expressionless.

"Who did you say did it?" asked Bradshaw.

"The one in uniform."

"Sure?"

"The other one was out in front with you, Mr. Bradshaw." There was a few seconds' silence.

"Well, *somebody* did it," Madge said, her black eyes fixed accusingly on Alice's face. Alice's heart sank.

"I'll take the suitcases up." Fred Bradshaw picked them up and trudged out of the room with them. Madge hastily went into the kitchen saying she would make the tea. Her face was pale and worried. She had no intention of being left alone with a deranged woman.

Alice heard Fred Bradshaw clumping from bedroom to bedroom with the cases, and the clatter as Madge filled the kettle.

She quietly opened the front door and let herself out and began to walk quickly from the house. Fred Bradshaw watched from a bedroom window as Alice hastened away. Then he came downstairs and joined his wife, and let out a sigh of relief.

"She's gone, thank God," he said.

"Poor woman," Madge said. "Nutty as a fruitcake." She locked the back door, then the French windows, then the front door and fixed the bolt and chain for good measure. "That should keep her out, if she tries to come back," Madge Bradshaw said.

"You wouldn't think it to look at her." Fred Bradshaw scratched his pink bald head again. He had a simple nature and was always unhappy when bemused.

"I don't get it, I just don't get it," he complained. "It is television that does it, if I've said it once I've said it a thousand times, too much tele, putting ideas into weak minds."

Madge readily agreed. "Yes, dear, you have certainly said it a thousand times. Perhaps more," she added acidly. "I was always against letting the place. It always leads to trouble. It's not worth it, especially not just for a week. And now we're cut off the phone." She stared at the dangling flex.

"Oh, for God's sake, Madge, stop going on about it!"

"I'm sure I shall not sleep easy tonight, with that crack-pot woman roaming around. I'll get you another cup of tea."

"Don't feel like it, thank you."

"What *do* you feel like?"

"Just a bit of peace and quiet," replied Fred Bradshaw sulkily.

CHAPTER 11

Alice's feeling of relief as she left the house was short lived. But she was sure she could not stay with the Bradshaws. It was clear that they thought she was mentally disturbed. Curtis and Alan must have put the idea into their minds, though she had to admit that her story was an unlikely one. But the insuperable fact was that "friends" of Curtis and Alan would be arriving shortly. Knowing nothing of the ambulance ploy she visualised a struggle and the inevitable end. And would they kill the unfortunate couple called Bradshaw because they had been witnesses? It seemed likely. She had to make a break for it.

It was possible, even likely, that Curtis might be waiting nearby with the soft voiced Alan, assuming that she would do just what she was in fact doing. Perhaps they were sitting in their car discussing what had gone wrong.

She fled round to the back of the house, and through the kitchen garden, past rows of onions standing like short sentinels, and past the scarlet flowers of tall runner beans till she came to a stile beyond which she saw a narrow winding lane. She climbed over the stile. The lane was so narrow that only one car could travel along it, but at intervals it was widened by cut-outs into which a driver could pull his car to allow an approaching vehicle to pass.

She had been half-running, but now she slowed down, partly because she was breathless, and partly to enable her to peer anxiously round each bend in the lane. Putting herself in their position she guessed that they might think she would avoid the front of the house in her flight, and would expect her to take the route she was indeed taking. Perhaps she should have left by the front. The more she thought about it, the more sure she became. But it was too late now.

She knew in her heart that even if she saw them before they saw her there would be little chance of escape. They would be after her like running dogs, and were stronger and faster. She was suddenly aware of the weakness in her legs produced by fear. She was staggering, swaying from side to side, but the weakness had to be overcome. She had to press onwards, no matter where to, so long as it put more distance between her and the house.

The lane joined a road, wide enough for cars to pass each other with ease. She saw one car pass and thought thankfully that she could probably hitch a lift in the direction of Melford, or even, with luck, all the way to Melford—if she knew where Melford lay. A signpost was visible at the junction of the lane and the road, and she ran hopefully towards it, only to find that some vandal had broken off the sides so that only the upright remained.

It was a bitter disappointment. But then, between some trees, she caught a glimpse of rising ground and a peak and guessed it was Gate Hill which loomed above Melford. She turned right and began to walk towards Gate Hill, unsteadily.

A big Rover car overtook her but the driver ignored her when she thumbed him for a lift. She was not surprised because it was filled with a family and luggage. Two other cars, driven by women, took no notice of her signals. A fourth car, a red Cortina, driven by a middle aged blond man, slowed down and stopped. She forced herself into an unsteady run and caught up with it.

"You all right, miss?" the driver asked.

"Could you give me a lift to Melford, please?"

The driver shook his head. "Not going that far, sorry."

"Well, to the next bus stop—do, please!"

"Last bus has gone on this route, miss."

"Well, to anywhere along the route."

"Hardly worth it, miss, I'm turning off a mile or two ahead."

"That would help, anywhere would help to get me away from this place, do please help," she pleaded. The driver suddenly looked solemn.

He had his hand on the gear lever and was about to engage first gear. He had light blue eyes and a healthy country complexion, and looked at her in a friendly way, and took his hand off the gear lever.

"You in trouble, miss?"

"Dreadful trouble. Please help me."

"Look, miss, whatever trouble you're in, you'll likely be in worse trouble if you try to hitch lifts in cars from strange men on their own. These are dangerous times, miss. What's the trouble, a bit too much to drink? You was walking a bit funny, I thought."

"I've been kidnapped, you've got to believe me!"

"Eh?"

"Kidnapped! They were going to kill me, but I escaped."

Alice's lips were trembling again, her voice piteous and pleading. The driver engaged first gear and looked at his wristwatch.

"Look, I'm late, miss, got to go. But there's a police car coming up behind me. You'll be okay with them, miss, two men in it. You'll be all right."

"You don't believe me, you think I'm drunk, but I'm not!" Alice cried. "Please stay with me, or let me go with you to wherever you're going. Please, please!" Her voice died away as she saw by the look on his face that she could not persuade him.

In her desperation she tried to open the passenger and nearside rear door but they were locked. She began to run round the back of the car intending to try other doors, and felt the heat from the exhaust pipe as she passed it. But she never reached the other side of the car. Before she could get to the other doors, the blond driver shouted something, and the Cortina moved away from her, slowly at first, then with gathering speed.

As it did so, a car traveling from Melford in the direction of the lane leading to the Bradshaw's house, drew up on the opposite side of the road. A man in the uniform of the Melford police force got out of the front passenger seat. He was a stocky middle aged man with iron grey hair which was not cut as trimly as one would expect to see on an old type police officer. Alice was tempted to run, but there seemed no point. The man adjusted his cap.

"You all right, miss?"

"I'm all right." The words came automatically. "I'm quite all right, at the moment."

"Taking a little walk, are you?"

"Just taking a little walk." The red Cortina had stopped a few hundred yards away. She saw the blond driver looking at them over his shoulder, watching the scene.

"Excuse me, miss, you've got an insect on the collar of your blouse. Keep still, I'll brush it off." He bent down and pretended to brush an insect off her collar, sniffing her breath. His eyes searched her face.

"Your gait was a bit unsteady, miss, sure you're not ill?"

"Quite sure."

She thought that if she could keep the conversation going some other car might come by: and another car did approach, swooping on them suddenly from around a bend. The male driver slowed but before she could make a decisive move, accelerated smartly, having decided that whatever was going on was none of his business, and he wasn't going to be mixed up in it.

She looked at the stationary Cortina, decided she would have one last try, and ran sobbing along the road towards it. But in her panic she tripped over an uneven part of the road and fell heavily. The man who was in uniform, waved to another man who nodded and got out, leaving the blue light on the car roof flashing, and ran towards them. He was not in uniform.

"You hurt, miss?"

"Not much," she replied, rubbing her grazed knee. A little blood had stained her torn stocking. "Anyway, what does it matter now?" she asked and meant it. They were not Curtis or Alan, but what did that matter, either? There were too many of them, their organisation and communications were too good. She could not fight any more, and she felt so weak that she doubted if she could even put up the good show which Ducane would expect.

"There's a first aid box in the car, miss. We'll give you a

piece of plaster for your knee. Just come along with us to the car." He helped her to her feet.

"Where do you live, miss?"

"In Melford. As if you didn't know!"

"We'll give you a lift to Melford, miss."

He put an arm round her to support her, and began to push her towards the car. She struggled to free herself, but the other man had joined them and was holding her firmly on the other side.

"I've been kidnapped once this afternoon. As if you didn't know," she said again, in a defeated tone. "Faked uniforms, faked police car, you're a well organised lot, you people, I'll say that for you. Expert killers, but you won't get Alexi Schorin, not through me." She babbled on, semi-incoherently. "Kill me if you like, but you won't get Alexi, not through me."

They had reached the car with the blue light flashing on the roof. She looked down the road. The red Cortina with the friendly but cautious blond driver was disappearing round a bend.

"Where are you taking me to?"

"General Hospital, miss, they'll give you an anti-tetanus injection, people ought always to have an anti-tetanus injection if they're hurt on a road. Might be infected by horse droppings, miss. It won't hurt."

"That's what Alan said about cutting off my finger. How is he, how's Curtis? How are your friends? I don't want an anti-tetanus injection—or any other kind of injection!" she protested, as they opened the back door of the car.

She struggled, still hoping that some other car with an inquisitive and more helpful driver might appear at the last moment. But she gave up after a few seconds. Men with a struggling woman and a police car, though interesting, would be no concern of other people. One man in uniform took the wheel, as Curtis had done, and his companion sat at the back with her, as Alan had done. As they approached Gate Hill they had to slow down. A flock of sheep, urged on by a man on a bicycle, blocked the road. Alice leaned forward and lowered the window at her side. She had no plan, but the sheep and the man represented normality. A wild idea crossed her mind. If she could open the door and fling herself out into the road among the sheep the man on the bicycle might do something; but what she did not know.

Any diversion was better than none, because any diversion meant a few more seconds of life, and the sight of sheep made her think again of a lamb being led to the slaughter. The man beside her fumbled in a side pocket, and she heard the click of handcuffs and felt the cold of the steel around her wrist. He must have guessed what might be in her mind.

"You don't need to do that," she objected feebly.

"It's just to protect you, miss. In case the door flies open and you fall out."

She slumped back and gave up. Anyway, she thought, Froggie Ducane would approve. By and large she had put up a good show—on the whole. Or if not a good show, at least the best of which she was capable.

She heard the sheep bah-ing as they passed on each side of the car in the quiet road, and the shouts of the man on the bicycle, and turned to watch them as they jostled onwards pushing and shoving each other, and thought that even sheeps' dirty behinds were a pleasing sight when life was short.

CHAPTER 12

In Brock's living-room they all raised their heads and looked towards the road as they heard the sound of a car engine, and the crunch of tyres on the road when it slowed and stopped. Brock caught a glimpse of headlights through a chink in the curtains and heard the rasp of a handbrake being applied. In the room was a stillness born of eager anticipation. Then the sound of the door bell, and small movements and relaxation due to disappointment: Alice had her own door key, and would have let herself in.

Another kind of anticipation was on Ducane's face after Brock had opened the door for him. He walked quickly into the room; Sugden followed him.

"Evening all," he said brightly. "I've been having a talk with ACC Tomkins, that's why I'm late. Why is he always in a state of indignation?" He looked round the room for Alice who was going to slip him the piece of paper on which she said she had written the name of Schorin's nestling.

"Where's Alice?"

"That's what I want to know," Schorin spoke loudly. "Where's my Alice?"

"You don't know?"

"No, and nobody seems to care."

Brock cleared his throat. "We think she's having a drink with a friend."

"It's you that thinks that. I don't." Schorin glowered at him.

"What do you think?" Ducane asked.

"I think she's had an accident or been kidnapped. He doesn't." Schorin waved a hand at Brock. "He's obstinate."

"She may have had an accident."

Ducane smoothed down the wisp of hair on the crown of his head. "Ring the hospital, that'll clear up one possibility."

Brock moved to the phone and dialled the hospital number and asked for the reception desk, and posed his question, and waited for a reply, and put down the receiver, and shook his head.

"No road accidents this afternoon. We are a law abiding community. We drive carefully."

Schorin snorted. "So what are you going to do?"

Brock pulled his long nose. "What do you want us to do?"

"Do! Search all lonely farms and buildings, alert your informers, and sea and airports, put up road blocks, stop all cars, just do something, ring all other hospitals, pull people in, ask questions." Schorin's speech was getting wilder, his suggestions more impractical.

"We'll wait till nine o'clock," Ducane said.

"Then what?"

Ducane ignored the question. "Who's Elliet?" he asked abruptly.

Schorin had been standing by the telephone, staring down at the instrument, as if wondering whether he could start some action himself. He swung round.

"Who's Elliet?" he repeated the question to gain time. Ducane glared at him.

"That's what I was asking—who's Elliet?" He was reasonably sure but wished that Alice had been present with her supporting evidence. But she wasn't, and secretly, so secretly that he did not yet admit it to himself, he was sharing Schorin's fears for her safety. Sugden broke the silence.

"Aye, the question's plain enough, isn't it? That's what Mr. Ducane here asked, you must be daft as a brush if you don't understand a simple question like that."

"Or boxing and coxing." Brock barked the words out. He guessed Sugden would not have been so insulting without tacit approval from Ducane.

"There is no Elliet," Schorin said with unexpected smoothness. "It is a made up name."

"He's floundering," Sugden said, "he's in a proper muck-

sweat." Ducane nodded. He was professionally astonished that
Schorin had apparently forgotten the cassette with its mention
of the name Elliet. Or had he forgotten? Probably not. Schorin
was lying, not a *vranyo* fun-lie, or a *lozh* scheming-lie, but perhaps a simple, instinctive, automatic lie. He sighed resignedly.
Dealing with Russians was like walking in boggy marshland, at
one moment the going seems firm and then suddenly it isn't.

Brock was not interested in the subtleties of Russian lies. He
surmised that peppery old Assistant Chief Constable Tomkins
had suggested that a confrontation was necessary. "Rough him
up a bit, if he won't play." Brock was glad Ducane had taken
the suggestion. He, too, was getting tired of Schorin's evasions.

"Or perhaps a slip of the memory? Can happen to anybody," Brock said.

"When it bloody well suits them," said Sugden, "that's when
it happens."

"Elliet, Elliet, always bloddy Elliet," grumbled Schorin. "What
about Alice?" Schorin shouted.

"Alice can take her turn," Brock said in a hard voice.

Schorin walked to the drinks cupboard as if to pour out another vodka, but stopped and changed his mind. He slammed
the cupboard door shut, face flushed with anger.

"No! First Alice!"

"Slippery." Brock looked at Sugden. "Shifty and slippery,
that's what he is." Brock was unconsciously reverting to his
old police technique when interrogating people. It always annoyed a suspect to be talked about as though he were not present.

Schorin put on a complaining voice. "You said these men
are my friends, you said they are to protect me, my friends, to
defend me! And now—"

"You said you came over to us because you were on our
side, lad," Sugden interrupted.

"Keeping stuff back, that's what he is," snapped Brock, ignoring Schorin.

"We defend our friends, aye, but is he our friend, we ask
ourselves?" Sugden sounded sad. "My friends don't keep stuff
back like who they know and who they don't. Not unless they
have something to hide."

They were still discussing Schorin as though he were not present. Schorin felt his anger continuing to rise.

"Loyalty to a friend is not to be despised," Brock remarked in the muffled voice he used to cool rising temperatures.

"Perhaps we could come to some agreement," Ducane said, "if we knew who Elliet is."

"Elliet might prove reasonable," Brock agreed, and blew his big nose with a sound like an angry elephant. "If we offered him immunity—in exchange for co-operation."

Schorin laughed. There was no amusement in the sound.

Jane Brock put her head round the door. "Supper's ready for anybody who wants it." Brock nodded, but nobody spoke, and Jane, sensing the atmosphere, softly withdrew and closed the door behind her, and went back into the kitchen and put the plates in the oven to keep warm. In the living-room Ducane had unlocked the heavy leather briefcase in which he carried delicate material when travelling. His office address was inside, and the theory was that if it were to be lost or found in a train, or after a car accident, some loyal citizen would return it or hand it in to the police. He often wondered if they would, or if they would throw the papers away and keep the handsome case. He took a couple of sheets of typescript out of the case, and glanced at them and said:

"Transcripts of the recording on the cassette which you gave Alice before you came over to us. Remember? We returned the original to you. It was the only thing stolen from the almshouse when it was broken into. Remember?"

Schorin nodded, his eyes watchful, guessing what was coming.

"Ukrainian and Georgian folk songs. Remember?" Schorin's heartbeat quickened as he prepared for the inevitable follow-up.

"And the end bit—remember it? Wishing everybody a happy day at Aldeburgh Avenue, including grandpa Elliet—remember?"

Schorin produced a carefully prepared smile. "Oh, him!"

"Yes, him—grandpa Elliet. Elliet," repeated Ducane.

"The old bookworm Alexis Schorin once wanted us to think does not exist," Sugden said and sniffed scornfully. He was en-

joying the confrontation. Alexis Schorin was not surprised at
the situation. He decided that attack was the best defence and
turned on Brock viciously.

"Why are you sitting there? Why are you not out looking for
my Alice?"

Ducane intervened: "Because I did not tell him to. We will
wait till nine o'clock. Then we'll think again. Is that clear?"
Alexis Schorin said nothing.

"Did we recognise the voice," Brock asked, "the one wishing
a happy day to this non-existent Elliet, and all the other little
pixies at Aldeburgh Avenue?"

"But of course it has been identified because it is my voice."

Schorin spoke gently and patiently now, and could have
been addressing a child who was not only innocent but also
thick and wooden headed.

"I checked the Aldeburgh Avenue house," Ducane admitted.
"There are no children there. There is a Robert Wagstaff Elliet
who lives alone and collects old books. Tell me more about
him. He is your friend." Ducane turned mild hazel eyes on
Schorin. "Tell me more about your friend, your nearly forgotten friend Elliet, do you forget your friends so easily?"

Schorin pretended to think, though there was no need to pretend. Disjointed thoughts chased one another through his mind
faster than they had ever done, one crowding out another before its predecessor had had time to mature. Elliet had to be
protected, because apart from Alice, Elliet—keeping his promise to Elliet—represented the last spark of loyalty and integrity
to which he could cling. True he had had to threaten Elliet,
but that was in Elliet's own interest. Elliet could not be and
would not be betrayed to Ducane.

"He *was* my friend," Schorin admitted at last and shook his
head. Time to grope about in the warm protection of vague-
ness, roofed over with truth. And half-truth. How much did
Ducane know, and Brock and Sugden guess? Not the final betrayal, not Elliet, his star nestling. So many names given to
Ducane, so many photographs identified. But no mention of
Elliet till now. Elliet was the raft.

"It was a shoke. The cassette talk—a shoke."

"A joke? For a friend? Tell me about your friend Elliet."

"He is a lecturer at a university."

"I know," said Ducane wearily. "I know that."

"And a teacher of French, German, and Russian."

"I know. How did you meet him?"

"When he was living in London."

"Mr. Ducane here asked *how* you met him," Sugden insisted, big head lowered, lower lip protruding.

"I advertised."

"You advertised for a spy?" Sugden's lips parted in a half-smile, his dark eyes gleamed. Schorin ignored him.

"I gave him lessons in Russian, he gave me lessons in English."

"By telephone, I suppose." Sugden sneered. "Him living near here, and you in London, or was it a postal course?"

Schorin fought to keep his temper. Something hard was in his stomach, like a hand grenade, only needing the pin to be pulled out, then would come the explosion. But preferably not yet, preferably not at all. Alice had once said his temperament would do him an injury one day, and he had nearly struck her, which would have proved it. But he hadn't. Where was Alice? He kept Alice in mind, because it helped to keep the pin in the hand grenade. The worry hurt but it helped.

"In London we met for lessons," Schorin muttered. "Then he did lectures round here. Then he started a language school. We wrote little essays, his in Russian, mine in English. And sent them to each other. We corrected them for each other. Sometimes he came up to London. To buy books, old books, attend book sales. Then too we exchanged essays."

"So I imagine." Ducane lifted one frog paw and began to tap the table. Tap-tap-tap. With three fingers.

"Old books are expensive," Brock said. "No doubt the language school was very profitable?" Ducane answered the question for him.

"Not very. In fact it lost money. Not surprising in this district."

"How do you know that?" The pin was getting loose in the hand grenade and Schorin's blue eyes were like hot ice.

"Friends in the Inland Revenue tell me things," Ducane said.

"Old books are expensive," Brock said. "So either he could not afford them or—"

"Or he was fiddling his tax returns," Sugden said. "This dear old friend was doing a tax fiddle."

"What kind of books does he collect?" Brock's question floated in the air, as light as a feather. Again Ducane answered for Schorin.

"Old history books dealing with France, Germany, Russia, England, all countries. Especially books dealing with military campaigns." Ducane got up and walked round the room with his springy gait. An ugly coiled spring, Schorin thought, not very froglike now. Except for the wide mouth in the sallow face.

"He had perhaps some other work?" Brock asked. Ducane sat down again, and said: "He had, he was military correspondent for a news agency."

"Oh, my God! That was years ago!" scoffed Schorin, and lit one of his few remaining Russian cigarettes. Brock had a hollow tooth which he had not had filled because he was afraid of the dentist. He picked at it now with a match end.

"What were his essays about?" he asked. "Gardening? How to prune roses? Football? Who was going to win the cup final? Or old military battles and campaigns?"

Jane put her head round the door again. "Are you or aren't you lot coming in to eat?"

"Soon," Brock said. "In a few minutes. I hope." He looked at her woodenly, eyes expressionless. She got the message and withdrew.

"The essays went to Moscow, via Alexis Ivanovich Schorin, didn't they?" Ducane said. Surprisingly, Schorin nodded.

"Look, it was this way." He produced the ingratiating tone he adopted when he wanted something. "They have these little magazines which pay well for small articles about interesting foreign things. He wanted the money, so—what harm done?"

"None, till he began to write about more modern wars I suppose?" Brock was still working on his hollow tooth, thinking reluctantly that Jane was probably right, he ought to have something done about it. Ducane was not impressed about the modern wars angle.

"Still no harm done, not in one way," he said. "But it's a classic recruitment tactic. It's called the honeycot approach. Good money for old rubbish, for catalogues, industrial handouts, published articles, stuff obtainable at trade exhibitions, all overt, nothing secret. Useless muck, really."

"Money for old rope," Brock said.

"Honey from old bears," Ducane grimaced. "Lots of it. Tastes nice. Easy, but habit forming. No danger. But addictive. Very addictive. Later the pot runs dry. No honey unless paid for. By instalments if need be, but paid for. Withdrawal symptoms very painful. Nasty side effects. Some can't take it. Craving too bad. Hooked."

Partly true, partly guesswork, thought Ducane, and where the hell was Alice? He'd made the checks he had told Schorin about. But if the cassette of good wishes were a joke, as Schorin had said, and if the rest of Schorin's story were true, what then? Ducane looked quickly at the defector. Honey for old rare books, he was sure of it, that was Elliet's weakness. Sugden was sure of it, too. And Sugden should know. During one of Elliet's occasional visits to London, Sugden had called at Elliet's house in Aldeburgh Avenue, and let himself in by the back door with one of his all-purpose keys. He had left the door ajar for a quick getaway if needed. And it had been needed because Elliet had not stayed overnight in London as he had told one of his language students he intended to do. And Sugden, gum-shoeing hastily out of the house, had been very annoyed. He said you couldn't trust anybody these days. "But books, I've never seen the like, not in a small private house. Shelves of 'em, in glass cases with curtains in front to keep the light out, leatherbound, most. Some in foreign languages. He must be barmy about 'em, a crank."

"Did you manage to fix the bleeper on his car?" Ducane had sounded anxious.

"Under the near-side rear bumper, before I went in." Ducane had looked relieved. If it were necessary to follow Elliet, the periodic ping of the bleeper could be followed at difficult moments and would be invaluable.

"I must confess," Brock now said in his most pompous official voice, "yes, indeed, I must confess I find it difficult to understand Mr. Schorin's attitude with his alleged alignment with our cause."

Schorin lowered himself into a chair and stared at his shoes. Sunk in Russian gloom, Brock thought, I believe he is going to crack if Jane doesn't come barging in. A big honey bee, working late, zoomed in from the garden, flew aimlessly round a bowl of flowers and departed. Schorin looked up and sighed.

"You don't understand," he said at last.

"That's what Superintendent Brock pointed out," Sugden said. "He doesn't understand, nor does Mr. Ducane here. Nor me, none of us understands." Brock made a dismissive movement with his right hand and Sugden did not elaborate. There was silence again. Then Schorin looked up.

"A man needs to be loyal to something or somebody. Even a defector does," he added.

"You could try being loyal to Mr. Ducane," Brock said, and instantly regretted saying it. Later he told Jane, in the privacy of the bedroom, that it was one of the silliest remarks he had ever made. Added to his normal insomnia the memory of it kept him awake half the night. It was, he thought, worthy of Sergeant Frost at his worst.

The remark had appalled Ducane and sent a searing jab through the dull headache which he had been trying to fight off all day with tablets; and he braced himself for the explosion he knew would come. He had not spent hours helping with the debriefing of Schorin without guessing at the emotional hand grenade which lay in Schorin's stomach. It was enclosed in home-sickness, and loneliness, despite Alice—and Alice was not even there now—plus disappointment at what Schorin considered broken promises. And guilt, the inevitable guilt. The euphoria had long since departed. The challenge had been met. And to a professional as experienced as Schorin, the smuggling out of documents, the location of cabinets and what was in them, the taking of wax impressions of keys and, more difficult, the testing of the reproduction keys, even the clandestine meetings with Ducane or Sugden, had presented few problems. The Zoo had been a good place to meet. Or a cemetery. He reckoned he had visited all the cemeteries in London. It was the testing of reproduction keys that he disliked most.

That and document copying. But the keys were what he really feared, because there was always the chance that they would jam in the lock and would be difficult to get out quickly. He had a cover story for most of his actions. But an explanation for being found coming out of a room where he should not have been in the first place, leaving a key jammed in a lock behind him, that was something which had always baffled him. In the event it had never happened. It had all been easy. Almost too easy. Very few exciting moments to mull over during the long, dull days of being debriefed, answering endless questions, of waiting for his naturalization papers and other documentation. Schorin was not a man who took kindly to waiting.

Ducane put his hand up to his aching forehead. Throb-throb-throb. He could have kicked Brock, despite his headache. The confrontation had come too quickly and not in a manner he would have wished. It was a game of chess, needing infinite patience to keep your temper and to keep the pieces on the board. A chess game with Russians could last days, weeks. He had to learn for certain who Schorin's undeclared agent was. He thought the nestling was Elliet. Alice thought she knew, but Alice wasn't there, and Brock, usually so good at things, had upset the chessboard. Sugden, who was not as thick as he seemed at first sight, tried to retrieve things.

"If Mr. Ducane here was told who your big nestling is, it would clear your friend Elliet, and other people, lad."

"Whose side are you on?" Brock asked again, making things worse.

"*Oh, for God's sake!*" Ducane had never before raised his voice when he had a migraine. It was painful enough to speak quietly. "Let it be, pipe down," he said in a quieter tone. It was too late.

Schorin leaped to his feet. Ducane knew the pin was out of the grenade. The last two tablets had not done much good. He fumbled in his pocket and took out another bottle of pain-killers, a different kind, and put two tablets in his mouth and began to chew them, not bothering to ask for water to help him swallow them. The explosion of the grenade was worse than even he expected.

"Bloddy hell!" shouted Schorin. Striding up and down the

room. Sensing danger, the danger mixed now with insults, not knowing what the danger was, only knowing the insults and injustice. The tablets were still bitter in Ducane's mouth. No effect yet. Kai Lung said, he who shares a cave with a tiger learns to stroke fur in the right direction. Brock hadn't learned it. Not about Russian fur. Blast Brock, blast bull-dozing Sugden. Blast them all.

"Bloddy, bloddy hell! Taking all, giving nothing, not even trusting, bloddy hell!" Round and round the room. First time round close to the walls, second time round a tighter circle, third time a still smaller circle, ending opposite Ducane. The others edging closer in, instinctively, protectively. Ducane had a shot in hand, but he didn't fire it yet.

Ducane looked up at Schorin. Poor Alice.

Schorin had swung away, seemingly intent on another tour of the room. He stopped, tall, and lithe. A thoughtful and crafty idea occurred to him. He looked suspicious and accusing. Then came a toss of the head, his mind made up, certainty written all over the handsome intelligent face. The danger, hitherto only sensed as something lurking in mist, was now apparent to Schorin, beyond all doubt, and the preception of it appalled him.

"Alice, oh yes, I see now! Very clever, very clever indeed!"

"What's clever?" Sugden asked. "I'm hungry."

"What's clever?" asked Ducane wearily. The long drive, the headache, the tablets he had taken, had combined to drain his strength and even, in some measure, his interest. The whole situation, the rage, the tantrums was almost unbearable, even allowing for Schorin's anxiety and Brock's unfortunate words.

"What's clever?" he asked again. "I wish I could think of something clever."

Schorin sat down. He kept repeating the word "clever" and nodding agreement with himself. Suddenly he made up his mind.

"I will tell you what is clever!"

"Go on, before you change your mind. Go on, jump, into the cold water, up to your ankles," Ducane said softly.

"I know why Alice is not here," Schorin said. "I know why you have not started a search for her! It is not the KGB who have taken her away, it is you who have taken her from me. You are holding her from me," Schorin said, still nodding. "You have kidnapped her, yes, in a manner of speaking we could say that.

"You will return her to me when I have told you the name of the one whom I will not betray. It is a useless weapon, *him* I will not betray. I promised *him* that, when I recruited him." Schorin had got to his feet again and was in full voice.

"All sorts of things I have betrayed—the KGB, the GRU, even agents, the Party, Russia—"

"Not Russia," Ducane murmured. "You said so yourself, not Russia—'Brezhnev and his corrupt regime,' yes, but not Russia."

The acrid taste of the tablets still furred his tongue. And his brain. That was the bad thing. There was a heaviness in his brain, the nervous system dulled, a tight band round his head. He rubbed his eyes gently, and thought of bed. There must be a bed he could hire, somewhere in Melford, away from everybody and everything. And a dark room without noise. No bright light, and no Schorin shouting. But the lights were bright in the room and Schorin was still shouting.

"Arrest me! I am not trusted! Arrest me, it is finished. You or the KGB have Alice. Alice is gone. Arrest me now and take me to the Russian Embassy. It is all over."

"I can think of easier ways of committing suicide," Sugden said.

"Perhaps I deserve it," Schorin said in an indistinct watery voice. "Perhaps I deserve it after the dreadful things I've done."

"I'll drive you up myself to the embassy in London tomorrow, if you like," Ducane snapped, because there had to be a real show-down, and it had to come before his own brain had become too fogged by pain-killing drugs. He took a sheet map out of the briefcase on the table and a list of names, with a cross against some of them.

"Smith. Bailey. Barnes. Parker. Two GRU. Two KGB victims. Revenge killings by your lot, I suppose. Since then three other GRU people have been taken care of since you came to Melford."

"Arrested? Was it necessary so soon? Did they know that I—?"

"Not arrested, just—gone."

"Disappeared? Gone abroad?" Ducane caught the note of hope and fired the last but one of his two shots.

"Gone abroad?" Schorin repeated his question. "Did they know that I—?"

"They probably guessed it."

"Gone abroad?" asked Schorin for the third time.

"Not gone abroad—dead," Ducane said bleakly, and saw the anguish and indignation in Schorin's pale face.

"You didn't need to kill them." Schorin was puzzled and angry, reproachful. "Unfair and unnecessary! Now I shall certainly go back, now I shall pay for the awful things I have done. And to hell with you bloddy lot!" Schorin's shouting brought Ducane's pain surging back.

"Not killed by us," Ducane said, voice dispassionate. "None killed by us." He picked a sheet of paper from his briefcase. "Police investigations reveal nothing to indicate a crime. Police surgeons reported no signs of violence. No wounds on bodies. Not even a cut. Contents of bodies contained no trace of poisons or injurious foreign bodies. Death from natural causes. Heart attacks. No inquests necessary."

He tossed the sheet of paper on to the table.

"Death from Formula Five, I suppose?" He looked Schorin full in the face, then, noting Brock's puzzled look, he said: "KGB Dirty Tricks department. Formulae Four and Six are normal. Formula Four—elimination by the bullet or bomb. Easily attributable to IRA or other terrorists. Formula Six—planned road accident. Jay walker killed by hit-and-run driver. Or car in ditch, smashed, smell of whisky, half empty bottle, all that. But KGB Formula Five, ah, that's different. That's one of the most ingenious things I've come across."

Ducane's admiration for Formula Five was obvious. "Schorin knows about Formula Five—don't you?"

"Yes, I know about it," said Schorin in a voice hardly above a whisper. "I have used it. Not in this country," he added hastily.

"It is something to be wondered at, an agent's dream come

true. Untraceable, and there is no protection against it, except to avoid it, and in the long run no means of avoiding it, and no antidote, and it leaves no trace."

Ducane's voice was lyrical in his praise. His headache had been temporarily banished. Brock looked shocked.

"Heart attacks, fatal heart attacks," Ducane said, voice flat and unemotional.

Brock was frowning, doubtful. "Formula Five—are you sure about it?"

Schorin answered for him: "Certainly it is true. KGB bastards use it. The GRU don't—not now. The formula is cowardly," Schorin said. For a while nobody made any comment.

"Smith, Bailey, Barnes, Parker, they all died of heart attacks —at suitable intervals of time, of course," said Ducane. "A beautiful weapon. None of your clumsy stabbing in the leg with the poisoned ferrule of an umbrella. Easy to carry, easy to use, wonderful invention. I don't think we have anything like it; if we have they haven't told me about it."

Ducane was still admiring, disapproving, and envious. Schorin noted the envy. His eyes were shining. Admiration for any Russian achievements still clawed at him, tugging, unwilling to free him completely.

"Itching powder!" Schorin said suddenly, going from the sublime to the ridiculous. Ducane had spread out the sheet map on the table, and had been underlining places and drawing a circle round them. But the enthusiasm in Schorin's voice made him look up.

"Very strong itching powder, Russians have that, too! Place some on the office chair, and it will work its way through the trousers! Not a killer, but it will keep a man away from his desk for a few days. Gain time to go through his papers, perhaps put a microphone in his room."

Schorin was excitedly explaining this wonder of Russian science. Volatile, unpredictable Schorin, thought Ducane, all talk of re-defecting gone, and thank God for the respite. No mention of Alice. Russia, Formula Five, itching powder, then perhaps Alice. So went the priorities, at the moment, in Schorin's mind. They are all the same, these defectors, Ducane thought again but Schorin was more so than most.

He would be glad when Schorin had gone. The novelty and triumph in the case had worn thin. Only irritation remained. Never knowing what mood he would be in, the need to think twice before speaking. The anxiety not to give offence. The need to stand firm. The desire to please. The necessity for an occasional slap on the wrist.

Damn and blast all defectors, no, not that, just God preserve me from having to cope with them, rehabilitate them, find them safe, well paid, prestigious employment in a land ridden with unemployment and vigilant unions.

Ducane was staring down again at the sheet map on the table and at the same time having a row with an imaginary shadowy critic who always seemed to be sneering at him: *"You try it, you damn well try it!"* Ducane wanted to say. He was looking at the map but still speaking mentally to the pin-striped supercilious shadow. *"See how long you last before you get a migraine, you try to cope with the steady trickle of Russians, Czechs, Hungarians, Bulgarians, Rumanians and Poles, fixing them up with national insurance, national health, birth certificates, marriage certificates, the lot, inventing cover stories to account for mythical pasts, and all without revealing too much. One false step, one misplaced confidence, one dead defector, and you risk halting the flow. You try it, brother, you just try it!"*

He was getting into a rage with the shadow critic—who remained unconvinced, he knew that. So did the defectors who grew tired of waiting. They never understood.

Ducane went on staring at the map trying to calm down. Schorin at least was leaving—with luck. And God help the Australians. They could have him, with a note: "From us Pommy bastards with love." It was a relief in more than one way. His list of managements who were willing to provide jobs without asking too many questions was getting thin. You couldn't plead for help too often. Patriotic appeals were fine— in moderation. Without moderation, managements got tired of seeing your begging face at the door.

Sugden's Yorkshire instinct had mostly kept him silent. See all, hear all, say nowt.

Ducane had taken a folding measure out of his pocket, of the kind carried by carpenters and other artisans, and unfolded it, and was using it as a ruler, drawing two lines on the map with a pencil.

"There were two other attempts on your men. I did not mention them because they failed. One in Birmingham, one in Bristol. Come over here," he said to Schorin, "come and look at these lines. One going from south-west to north-east, one from south-east to north-west." Schorin came over to him, and looked down over his shoulder. Ducane pointed to the lines.

"See where they converge, see where they cross? In or near Worcester. Perhaps in Aldeburgh Avenue. Why not? Anywhere in Worcester on this small scale map. Why not Aldeburgh Avenue?" He watched as Schorin pursed his lips. Then he leaned back in his chair and said: "I think Elliet is your key agent, the one you are so coy about. I think he is in great danger. I think he would be safer in one of our prisons, guarded day and night. Not entirely safe, never that, but safer, much safer. Then we could talk, Elliet and I, then perhaps I could do something for him, get him to a safe place. Like Australia."

Schorin said nothing. Some of his bronze coloured hair had fallen over his forehead when he leaned over Ducane's shoulder to look at the map. He was on the point of saying, "I am not a horse to be tempted by that sugar," but he brushed back the hair from his face and said nothing.

"He is in great danger," Ducane insisted. "In my view it is impossible to exaggerate the danger. They are wiping you out."

He pointed at the lines on the map. "They are eliminating the GRU, your network, one by one. Brezhnev and his lot will give the present GRU funds to the KGB. More money, more influence, there will be no stopping them, they will rule Russia, they will eat up even Brezhnev and his crowd in the end, they will be the masters for a long, long time. Perhaps for any foreseeable time. Elliet is one of yours, I know it, I cannot prove it, but I know it. Give me evidence to pull him in, to save him! Your former friends, the GRU, are hitting back but they are losing."

Ducane's voice died away. He saw the look on Schorin's face, and guessed it was a hopeless struggle. He thought that Schorin was a fool, that quixotic loyalty could be self-defeating, that the main end had to be kept in view. He glanced round the room. Brock, the flexible superintendent, might accept that, obstinate Sugden probably would not, nor would Schorin with his mixture of Russian ruthlessness and Russian sentimentality. Most people had their pet loyalties. Rocky chips in uncertain sands, some big, some mere pebbles, small piles of pebbles, carefully guarded in normal times, reluctantly discarded. Schorin had flicked most of his pebbles away, till of all the pebbles only Alice and Elliet remained, cupped in Schorin's hand.

A discreet run-down on Elliet's character by a university professor who knew him had yielded little: "Highly intelligent, quick-witted. Interested in history and old books, especially those dealing with wars. Member of the Conservative Party." (Well, he would be, would't he?) "Politically expresses right wing views, if any." (He would, indeed he would.) Interrogation? About what? A search of his house? Likely to produce what? Nothing, except valuable books. Too intelligent to fall into that trap.

"Give me some evidence, for his sake," Ducane pleaded in a dull tone. "It could save his life."

"No!" Schorin's voice exploded in the room like a cannon shot.

"Don't shout," Ducane said. "It hurts my head."

"I don't know what you're talking about, you waste your time and mine." Schorin looked at a clock on the wall. "Nine o'clock, time to start the search for Alice."

Brock had moved to the settee. Sugden sat on a chair in the shadows in a corner of the room.

"Shall I push him around?" Sugden looked hopefully at Ducane. Ducane shook his head. A voice inside Ducane whispered urgently, above the noise of the throbbing, above the ticking of the clock on the wall. Shoot now, hunter with a headache. The shot was to have been a *feu de joie,* a signal for celebration. Congratulations. Drinks all around. Everybody happy. And good news for Schorin. Now it was different.

Ducane put a hand on his briefcase lying on the table, slim fingers and thumb were spread out like a predatory paw.

"Your naturalization and other papers have arrived," he said, and took them out of the briefcase, and laid them on the table.

"Also two air tickets for you and Alice. You fly the day after tomorrow, all being well." Schorin stared at the papers, making no move to take them.

"They've been a bloddy long time coming," he said ungraciously.

"It is a question of security," Ducane explained patiently, forcing the words out, struggling to keep his temper. "Naturalization in your own name would not have been difficult, but building up a false identity, with a new name, with supporting documents, that takes care and time. Faking social documents and passports is illegal and—it's been quick, considering the precautions which had to be taken. In this small island—"

"Yes, it is small," jeered Schorin. "And your own show is small, and bloddy slow, in Russia they would have had these papers ready for me." He put out his hand to take them.

Ducane, froglike, could move fast enough when he had a mind to do so. There was a splat sound as his right hand came down sharply on the papers on the table, and a rustle as he clawed them back out of Schorin's reach, and a hard mean look in his eyes. He was fed up with the rudeness, tired of the complaints.

"All right, we'll play it the Russian way! We'll do some trade. Tell me more about Elliet. Otherwise no papers." Ducane began to put the papers back into his briefcase. "We'll play it the Russian way," he said again. "You admire Russian ways, go on admiring them. In Russia it's played with Jews and exit visas. Over here, in your case—you see what I mean, don't you? You do see what I mean?"

The documents were back in the briefcase. He tugged at the zip and closed the briefcase and looked up at Schorin.

"I agree with you, there is much to be said about Russian ways."

"You can't do that, that is not legal, you are stealing from me papers that are mine!"

"They should have taught you British law. The Home Secretary can grant British nationality—and the Home Secretary can withdraw it if he sees fit."

He did not know if it was true. It probably wasn't. He had known of no case where it had happened, but it didn't matter. It was all go, at the moment, no holds barred. "I know the Home Secretary personally," he added for good measure. "Shall we talk about Elliet?"

Although he had only just put the papers back he opened the briefcase again and took them out and laid them on the table.

"What about Alice?" Schorin said, staring at the papers on the table. "Elliet this and that, what about my Alice? It is past nine, and you do nothing about Alice."

"Tell me about Elliet."

Ducane's forehead was glistening. He was over-heated by a combination of the hot evening and the pain-killing tablets. He would like to have opened the window shutters and let air into the stuffy room. But he did not dare to do so. Schorin would be an easy target.

He now shared Schorin's fears for Alice. She should have been back by now, or have telephoned. And because fear and apprehension are infectious and feed and breed off their own bodies, his anxiety to get Schorin out of the country had also suddenly grown. Beneath his air of confidence he felt the danger which was all the greater because it could not be pinpointed.

Schorin again made to grab the documents and Ducane let him take them. Brock frowned his disappointment.

Schorin's face showed no excitement or pleasure. His blue eyes were cold. He had the documents and he had the revolver Brock had disapproved of. Nothing mattered now, not even life. Inured to treachery, trained in deceit, nothing surprised him, not even Ducane's blackmail. In the surprised silence which followed after he had snatched the documents, disjointed thoughts and plans once more began to whirl through his mind, till finally they were reduced to two. The two pebbles of loyalty had been all he had left.

Alice was gone, and life would be pointless without her. Always on the run, until they got him in the end, as they would, with gun or with a toxic smear and a heart attack. Without Alice there was no incentive to take care. Blankness, a desert, nobody who minded, nobody to love.

Alice had gone but a man had still to try to be loyal to something or somebody. Only Elliet now was left.

He did not love Elliet, and Elliet did not love him. The promise: "I will never betray you." Others, yes, they took their chance as they took their money. Only Elliet remained, the last and the most important of the nestlings. The first of them, too, hand reared, trained, and cosseted, not only because of his value as an agent, but because of the fine brain. It was an honour to be treated as a friend by Elliet. As valuable as a nugget of gold.

From across the Close came the sound of the cathedral clock striking the half-hour. It was echoed by the small grandmother clock in the hall of Brock's house. A clatter in the kitchen opposite showed that Jane Brock, impatient, was washing up the frying pan and the cooking utensils she had used to prepare the meal which nobody had yet eaten.

What followed the silence was never fully explained. But neither is a sudden change of wind when a warm mild zephyr turns into a cold gusty squall. Alice might have come close to explaining the convolutions of Alexis Schorin's emotions and actions, but Alice was not available. It seems more likely that it was a combination of anger and vodka which prompted him to act as he did.

"No!" Schorin said in a loud voice.

He tore the documents twice, once from top to bottom and then at right angles, quartering them, and threw the pieces on to the table in front of Ducane. "Keep your bloody documents!" he shouted. Brock broke the astonished silence.

"That was silly, wasn't it? It took a lot of work to get you properly documented. A lot of pushing and influence and now—"

He did not finish the sentence. Even if he had tried to, his words would have been drowned by the loud pounding at the front door. Schorin reached automatically for the gun under his left shoulder. Apart from that, nobody moved, and nobody spoke, each silently looking at each other. After a few seconds the pounding was repeated, and more loudly. They heard the kitchen door open as Jane came out to go to the front door. Sugden leaped to intercept her.

"I'll go, lass, you get out of the passage."

He went to the front door. Brock followed him, waving at Schorin to keep back.

CHAPTER 13

On the way to the door Brock pushed past Sugden. "I'll open it, you give me some back-up, just in case."

In case of what? He didn't know. It was one of those evenings. He thought that menace, in one form or another, stood on the other side of the door, and Melford was his patch, he was responsible for it, and not these types from Whitehall who barged in, descending out of the blue, without warning, bringing nothing but trouble.

A third pounding on the door, impatient and peremptory, confirmed his belief that nothing peaceful stood on the doorstep. He glanced briefly over his shoulder as he put his hand on the doorknob. Sugden was frowning, head lowered, bull-like, tense and expectant. Brock pulled the door wide open with a sudden jerk, standing slightly to one side, on the balls of his feet, ready to jump whichever way circumstances dictated.

A glance at the flat checker-board cap and Melford police uniform of Sergeant Johnson told him he had been wrong. Johnson was apologetic.

"Sorry to trouble you, sir. I have a young lady in the car," he murmured. "She is in a distressed condition, sir. She alleges she knows you."

His tone was phlegmatic, but implied that he found that unlikely. He hurried on, anxious to excuse himself for what he clearly considered to be an unwarranted intrusion into Superintendent Brock's privacy, and at an inconvenient time.

"While proceeding along the Melford-Worcester road, sir, PC Dale and I observed a young woman walking towards Melford. Her gait being unsteady, I instructed PC Dale to stop and I asked her if she needed assistance. She shrank away and appeared to be making some attempt to elude me. I detained her, stating that I was a police officer. She appeared to be in an emotional state and replied that she had been kidnapped by a person wearing Melford police uniform and another person in plain clothes, but had managed to escape from them." The sergeant's droning voice died away as he paused to draw breath.

"Where is she?" Brock asked urgently.

"In the back of the car, sir. Handcuffed to PC Dale, sir."

"Handcuffed!"

"Yes, sir. When we invited her to enter the car, for further discussion, as it were, she became violent. Her breath did not smell of alcohol, sir, as we thought it might, but we formed the impression that she might be mentally disturbed. We therefore took her into custody for her own protection and to avoid any action by her which could have caused a breach of the peace. It was our intention to transport her to Melford General Hospital, sir, but in view of her repeated demands to be taken to you, we reluctantly agreed, sir. I trust we did right, sir?"

"You did right. Bring her in, sergeant."

"If you say so, sir."

There was doubt in his voice, but he was relieved to be rid of her, and it would be worth a few drinks in the canteen. He turned round and shouted, "Take the bracelets off, Bill, and bring her in."

They watched as Dale did as he was ordered, and Alice walked slowly up the garden path. Once she stumbled and the officer supported her for the last few yards. In the passage Schorin shouted, "Alice," and ran to her. Ducane stood watching from the living-room. He looked as bemused as the rest of them. Jane came in and looked at Alice.

"You're a bit late," Jane said, slightly reproachful. "Supper's ready."

Alice peered at her, eyes blinking in the light after the darkness outside.

"I don't feel like food," she said. "Just a large gin and tonic."

Five minutes later while she was drinking her gin and tonic, hand still shaky, giving uncertain replies to the questions flung at her, the telephone on the shelf behind her suddenly called for attention, angry and demanding as usual, like a spoilt child.

She remembered how it had shouted at her in the early hours
of the last night she and Alexi had spent in Ebury Street, when
Kuznetsov had telephoned Alexi.

The present jarring intrusion shattered her feeling of relief at
being back, at seeing Alexi safe, and her enjoyment of being
secure among friends.

Brock swore and answered the phone, dropping a clean
handkerchief into Alice's lap as he made his way to the instrument, because the sudden noise behind her had made her jump
and slop some drink on to her skirt.

"Somebody speaking from a call box," Brock said when he
had replaced the receiver. "He wanted to speak to you, Alexi.
He wouldn't say who he was. I told him to go to hell, as you
heard. He's rung before, earlier in the evening."

"Who was it?" Alexi asked, and knew it was a silly question.

"How do I know, he didn't say."

"How did he know I was here?"

"I don't know."

Ducane looked at Brock. "Tell the exchange to monitor all
incoming calls and record them."

"Phone tapping," Brock sighed. "Melford, the Poor Man's
Watergate."

"I know the Home Secretary, he's a personal friend," Ducane said for the second time that day. Brock nodded. But as
he moved to the phone it rang again.

"Let it ring. I think we'd all better go in and eat," Brock said
firmly.

"I don't feel hungry," Alice objected.

Schorin was sitting by her side on the settee, his arm round
her shoulders. He shook her gently.

"I think you ought to try and eat something."

"All right, I'll try."

In the corner of the room the phone was still ringing.

"I think you should answer it," Ducane said. "Or take the
receiver off the hook before it drives us mad. But I think you
should answer it." Brock got to his feet, reluctantly, and went
to the phone.

"Hello? Superintendent Brock speaking."

He felt hungry and irritable and his mood was reflected in

his voice. After a couple of seconds he put his hand over the mouthpiece and nodded at Ducane.

"It's the same bloody man. He wants to speak to Alexi," he said in a loud whisper.

"Play along with him. See what he wants." Ducane mouthed the words rather than spoke them, but Brock understood.

"He's not here," Brock said into the mouthpiece. He listened for a few seconds, then spoke impatiently. "He's out. No, I don't know where he is." Brock made a gesture with his right hand indicating that he wanted a pencil and something to write on.

Ducane snatched a ballpoint pen from his pocket and a pad of paper from the table and loped across with them, eyes gleaming. Brock swept an ashtray from the ledge where the phone stood, to make room for the pad, and the ashtray fell to the carpet scattering its ash and three or four of Schorin's long Russian cigarette butts.

"No, I don't know when he will be back, and anyway who are you? Yes, it does matter. A friend? Speaking for other friends? What friends? I didn't know he had any friends." He turned and winked at Schorin. "Well, the next time you call, if you do, I'll treat it as a nuisance call, is that clear? A nuisance call, that's what I said. I'll have this line monitored. What? Yes, all right I'll take a message for him, if you make it short."

Brock pulled at the pad of paper and began to scribble hastily. Occasionally he said, "Yes," and now and again he asked the caller to repeat his words. Finally he said, "I don't know what the hell you're talking about, I hope Mr. Schorin will. He will? So much the better. And stop cluttering up this line, it may be needed for something urgent. What? Yes, well, the message doesn't sound urgent to me. But I'll pass it on."

There was a click as the caller rang off. Brock replaced the receiver, and looked down at his hurriedly scrawled notes, trying to decipher and make sense of them. Then he turned round.

"It's a message for you, Alexi. Whoever it was had a local accent—I think—and he said that unless you went voluntarily to the Soviet Embassy in Kensington, London, and asked to be allowed to go back to Moscow—"

"Allowed?" Ducane's wide thin lips were compressed into a semblance of a smile. "*Allowed* to go back—that's good, that is!"

"It's what he said." Brock was looking down again at his notes. "Unless you gave yourself up, that's what he meant, then it would not go well for Alice *next* time. That's what he said." Brock's voice trailed away.

Alice felt Schorin's strong arm tighten so hard round her shoulders that it hurt, and she winced. Brock coughed, cleared his throat, and said: "He said something had gone wrong this afternoon, but she wouldn't be so lucky a second time. He didn't explain, he said Alice would know what he meant. He said kidnapping was easy, in the long run there was no protection. That's what he said to say to you, Alexi."

Schorin was breathing heavily. Alice felt his grip round her shoulders tighten again, but this time she did not wince. Gazing up she saw his eyes, loving, yet hard and determined. She managed to free one arm and reached up and stroked his hair.

"Take no notice, darling," she whispered, "I'll be all right."

"No!" Schorin suddenly shouted. "You won't be all right, and I won't be all right."

"Then we'll go together, my love."

"No," shouted Schorin again. "My nestling was loyal, but I might at the last moment have changed my mind and let him take his chance with the rest of the GRU in this war with the KGB. But you are different, little Alice. You can change your name and go to another country and maybe live, and I will go back to Moscow."

He bent down and kissed Alice. Ducane caught Brock's eye, and affected to stifle a yawn.

"Tale of two cities situation, it's a far, far better thing that I do now than I've ever done before. I can't bear it, I've heard it all before," Ducane murmured. But despite his words he was more worried by Schorin than ever before.

He had an uneasy feeling that Schorin was now in earnest; and a tantalising feeling that he might still stop Schorin in his tracks if he could only find the key to make this temperamental Russian think again. Schorin was prolonging his kiss, as if he were saying a last goodbye before facing a firing squad.

Ducane was feverishly raking over old memories, back to the days when he was worried about the motive for Schorin's defection, whether it was genuine or the ploy of a double agent. The key lay somewhere there, but he couldn't find it. Schorin was already pushing Alice gently away.

For a few seconds she resisted, and clung to him, but in the end she gave in and allowed him to release her. Apart from anything else Schorin's long, strong hug was making her gasp for air. It was while she was groping for a handkerchief in her handbag that Ducane remembered something Alice had said about Schorin. It was a long shot, and Ducane had little faith that he would hit the target. But he fired it.

He smoothed down the tuft of hair on his scalp. His smile was so wide that the two ends of his mouth seemed likely to meet at the back of his head but his voice was soft and sneering.

"So it was all bluster and boasting," Ducane said, looking at Schorin with mocking eyes. "Big talk, eh? And nothing behind it. A sort of twisted and distorted *vranyo*."

Schorin leaped to his feet and seemed unable to believe his ears.

"What was big talk?" Ducane took no notice of him. Ostentatiously ignoring him, he looked at Brock and said: "All talk and no action, didn't I say that, right at the beginning?"

"Empty vessels make the most noise," Brock agreed, and stroked his big high bridged nose. He guessed what Ducane was up to, and had no more faith in it than Ducane. But if Froggie Ducane wanted to play it that way it was okay with him.

"Likes a challenge, that's what Alice once said in the early days," Ducane said.

He gave an audible sigh and looked at Schorin. "Tell your chief nestling he's on his own. If we don't get him the KGB will. You promised to protect him. You can't now. He's a goner. Same as you will be. It's your choice. Same as Alice will be, when you're not around. She's no good on her own. Kidnapped in Melford in broad daylight! Hopeless."

Schorin thumped the table making the glasses and ashtrays

jump. "I'll go to Australia with Alice—for a while—then I'll be back and carry on."

Ducane caught Brock's eye again and they both smiled slightly. Each knew what the other was thinking, and they were not smiles of triumph. Each was thinking the same thing: I hope to God this charming but turbulent man will *not* be back. Let the Australians have him.

Schorin did not notice the smiles. He was staring down at the torn up naturalization papers and air tickets on the table. Alice looked dismayed, too. Ducane followed the line of her eyes.

"Naturalization papers," Ducane said. "He tore them up."

"More delay," Alice said sadly. "We could have been away soon."

"The day after tomorrow," Ducane said. "You still can."

"I don't get it."

Ducane pointed to the torn up documents. He looked smug. "Photo-copies, dear, and very good ones, too. They do a good job at the office when they have to. They ought to," he added sourly, "considering the practice they get. I dropped off the originals with the Assistant Chief Constable on my way here this evening."

Alice looked at Schorin, her grey eyes shining. Jane put her head round the door.

"Are you lot going to eat or aren't you?"

Alice said, "I'm hungry, too, now."

She motioned with her head to Schorin and Brock, but detained Ducane with a glance when he made to follow them. When they had gone out of the room she whispered to Ducane: "Elliet of Aldeburgh Avenue, near Worcester. Mentioned on the cassette. Alexi talks in his sleep. Mentioned him twice in Ebury Street. Forgot to report it. Said nothing of importance about him."

"No proof, nothing against him," whispered Ducane. "Just an old book lover and language teacher. Hasn't seen him for years."

Alice shook her head. "Why send a joke cassette if they weren't still very friendly?"

Ducane shrugged his shoulders. But he filed her words in the card indexed information in his mind. He and Alice joined the others for the delayed meal.

Alice was still happy.

Everybody seemed happy as they sat at table and ate their supper. Each realised that it was likely to be the last time when they would all be eating together. Curiously enough each felt an undertone of regret at the thought, though none would have admitted it. Brock, too, was pleased that he would be able to get back to the humdrum duties of a provincial police superintendent and to the peaceful life he had sought when asking for a transfer from Northern Ireland.

Ducane, practical as ever, was sorry that he was to be deprived of a handy source of reference; but, as the man mainly responsible for Schorin's safety, he was pleased by the prospect of the burden being lifted. For a few seconds he baulked at recognising the doubt which niggled at the back of his brain, but knew he had to face it.

Finally he did face it. If he *does* get away alive, he thought uneasily. Much could happen in two days.

For Alice the dream of shortly having Alexi to herself, in relative safety, in a distant sunny land, was unmarred even by the necessity to have to say farewell to relatives in England. She had none. She was already planning what clothes she would have to take. If the general mood of gaiety was a trifle forced and superficial it was not for want of efforts made by everybody. Even Sugden tried his best when Schorin disappeared from table and came back with a bottle of red wine.

"Bull's Blood, let us drink to happiness, now we are all happy!" Schorin cried.

"Except the bull," murmured Sugden. A small, heavy little joke, but his own, Ducane thought, and raised his glass.

Brock fixed up a room for Ducane at the Blue Boar. They all went to bed early, all problems seemingly solved. Alice did not stay awake long. Reaction, gin, food, wine and happiness did their work, added to the fact that she and Alexi were now safe in Brock's guarded home. All was well.

Jane was still irritated by the lateness of the supper. In her sturdy Scottish mind good food was essential and should be eaten punctually at regular times, but she soon slept.

Brock worried for a while as to whether the police guard on the house was in place and alert. Once he got up and noiselessly walked to the window and looked out. Moonlight flooded the road and the houses opposite. About fifty yards away he discerned the dim figure of a man standing in shadows by a wall. As he watched another man approached. The two stood talking, and he saw the red glow of cigarette ends. For various reasons Brock did not approve of officers smoking on duty. But at least it kept them awake. Satisfied, he went back to bed and was asleep in an unusually short time. Ducane, heavily drugged, also slept peacefully.

Only two people were awake at midnight in the moon-drenched quiet house in Sheldrake Drive: Sugden and Schorin.

Sugden, outwardly so obstinate and unemotional, periodically turned his heavy body from side to side as he engaged in his nightly struggle with guilt, hearing Rachel Levin's voice, "All right, darling, if you're sure that's what you want," seeing her walk out of the restaurant in Earls Court Road, pushing past the stained tables to the door, without glancing back. Her self-inflicted death was not what he wanted or expected. Useless to tell himself over and over again that she was wrong. He would willingly have traded all his bachelor freedom and much else, to reverse the train of events, and give her back some years to add to her life. Sometimes, in the darkness, he tried to tell her so. But tonight the only response he got was the memory of the tatty little dinner bill and the banknote she had hidden beneath it as a contribution to the cost of the dinner.

He told himself, as usual, and with the same result, that what was done was done, and it was all over. But it wasn't. And never would be, and he knew it. He was aware that people wondered why he was unmarried, or at least not shacked up with a woman to look after his needs. But in the end even Sugden slept. That, at least, would bring no sense of guilt in the morning and was what Rachel would wish.

Soon after midnight only Schorin was awake. The cathedral was still bathed in soft blue light because there had been another rehearsal for the forthcoming Day of Expiation pageantry. The rehearsal had gone on longer than usual, and nobody had yet switched the lights off.

He realised, now, that Ducane, the crafty frog, had needled him with his talk about the KGB winning, in order to stop him from re-defecting. So bloddy what? He would go to Australia, but he would come back one day. Alice would have to be more careful. That did not apply to him, he was always careful, he could always look after himself. Alice had once called him her young tiger, and now the rôles were reversed. The tiger would have to train the keeper.

He foresaw no difficulty in leaving in two days' time. The sooner the better. Action, even danger, was better than sitting around doing nothing. The decision to go, and the cheerful atmosphere of the last part of the evening, had been wholesome. He knew that he had sometimes been drinking too much since his defection; and before it, come to that, when he had been secretly helping Ducane. He liked vodka, but he knew that he had been trailing wisps of guilt around for a long time, and the vodka had helped to disperse the recognition of the extent of his betrayals. Now it was over, now he was committed, now there need be no more heavy drinking.

Brock, the badger-like policeman, had left books by his bedside, including verse by some Persian poet, an old drunk. He remembered some lines because they seemed to apply to himself, "Indeed, indeed, repentance oft before, I swore, but was I sober when I swore?" He was sober now. And he swore: some vodka, but not much. There was no need for it.

All doubts gone, he thought, and remembered Elliet, the man who had had so many brilliant if undramatic triumphs in the field of acquiring difficult documents. Elliet whom he had never betrayed, despite pressure from Ducane. He remembered how, in his moods of guilt, the thought that he had always kept his promise to Elliet had been a consolation, a sop to his conscience. He had no doubt that sometime in the future Ducane, or one of his men in Australia, would try again to make him break his promise. They would have no success.

He knew he would have to see Elliet before he left for Australia, and explain the unexpected developments. Otherwise Elliet would be worried by the lack of contact. His deeply ingrained agent-running instincts would not allow that. One must part on good terms with an agent, never let him down, never run out on him. Anyway, he needed Elliet to help him write his book. He was not going to run out on him, nor should he give that impression, not ever, for however short a time. He would have to see Elliet tomorrow, the day before he and Alice left the country.

He looked at the cathedral and nodded agreement with himself. As he was looking at the cathedral the floodlights were suddenly turned off, abruptly and totally. The moon had dipped behind a thick bank of clouds, the street lamps had also been switched off. Melford was in darkness. There was no indication that any evil would be afoot when dawn broke.

CHAPTER 14

Standing in the phone box near Brock's house, Schorin waited what seemed a long time when he rang Elliet early the following morning. In his experience callers gave up too soon when they tried to phone people. First, there might be a long wait till the phone was heard, then a wait while they came from wherever they were, perhaps the garden.

He had never liked phone boxes, had liked them even less since Kuznetsov had been gunned down in the phone box in Ebury Street. One was exposed in a phone box. He had brought his automatic with him, and it lay on the coin box, covered by a handkerchief, but if it came to a show-down he had no illusions about what his chances would be. They would fire first. It must be so. He could hardly shoot at any passer-by who paused suspiciously by the box to make a call. Even Ducane would not cover that one up, and Brock the policeman would certainly not wear it. So he stood for several minutes anxiously looking out of the box and wishing Elliet would answer more quickly. In the end Elliet answered.

"I have to see you," Schorin said briskly.

"When?"

"This morning."

"I have an appointment."

"Cancel it." Schorin spoke in a sharp way which Elliet had never heard before.

"Where?"

"Roman bridge."

"On the bridge?"

"Course not!" Schorin's voice was impatient. "Usual rendezvous nearby. Eleven-thirty."

"In the conifer wood, in the hut?"

"Yes."

"Is it really urgent?"

"Top Urgency. You know what that means."

"My appointment concerns my job, being taken on again, all that."

"This concerns your life."

"Okay, I'll be there." Schorin heard the phone click at the other end. He looked cautiously round. Nobody was near, and he returned to Brock's house for breakfast, his conscience clear. Alice looked up as he came into the kitchen.

"Where have you been?"

"Having a stroll in the sunshine. I have to leave you this morning." She looked at him, a panicky expression on her face.

"Don't! Please don't go out till tomorrow! Please don't leave me!" He shook his head and went round the table and kissed the nape of her neck.

"I'll be back for lunch." She looked at him with pleading eyes. "Where are you going—and why?"

"Not far, little Alice. Just to place a few flowers on the grave of an old colleague," he lied. Any story would have to do for her.

She pushed her half eaten meal away from her. "I'll wait for you before I eat lunch. I'll wait for you forever," she said mournfully.

Schorin went out. He still had the keys of an office car, a small Allegro, and unlocked it and drove away. The others joined Alice later, and heard what had happened. Nobody commented. To break the disapproving silence Jane told Brock that apparently there was something wrong with the electric wiring of the house. A man had called to mend it. He said the fault also affected the phone box down the road.

"Did he identify himself?" Ducane's voice was quiet. She shook her head. "I—well, I didn't ask him." Jane went out of the room. They heard the click of the telephone, and her voice, but could not hear what she said. When she came back she looked puzzled and worried. "They say they have no record of any of their people calling here on a job."

"Did they trace the fault?" Sugden asked. She nodded.

"He wasn't here very long." She tried to sound cheerful. And hopeful.

"Did he trace it and repair it, lass?" She nodded again.

"So where was it?"

"In the wainscoting in the living-room," she answered, and her voice was hardly above a whisper.

"Oh, my God," Sugden said and put both hands to his head, covering his eyes in a rare gesture of despair. He left his breakfast half uneaten and went out and phoned Ducane.

Schorin thought briefly of Sam Letts as he drove over the Roman bridge to where he always left his car on his assignments with Elliet, and made his way to the small wooden hut. He opened the door, saw Elliet, and stood in the entrance surveying the countryside around him.

"What are you looking for—Special Branch types?" Elliet asked, after a full two minutes. A gathering breeze stirred the conifers around the hut.

"Not Special Branch, KGB," Schorin replied. Elliet seated himself at a rough little table, his briefcase in front of him, and Schorin sat down opposite, and described the course of events. Schorin took out his automatic and shook out the bullets and blew through the barrels to make sure they were clear. He had not cleaned it for some time, and did so now as fast as he could with a pocket handkerchief.

"*Now don't put them back,*" ordered Elliet, opening his briefcase. "KGB you want? Looking for KGB? You don't need to look far," he said and carefully took out his own gun from the briefcase. "I'm sorry it has to end this way." There was a ring of truth in his voice as he raised his Walther automatic.

"I'm sorry, too," Schorin said. His blue eyes were cold and merciless as he fired and saw the dark red hole in Elliet's left forehead, and he was glad he had been taught quick accurate snap-shooting in the old days.

He carefully wiped the five live bullets with his handkerchief and the used one, and his Lüger, and, hardly glancing at Elliet, he wiped the Lüger again and pressed it into Elliet's hand before placing it on the floor near Elliet's face. He took Elliet's Walther and put it in his own holster.

Now there is only one left, he thought, and she is waiting for me, and will wait for me forever. Or so she says. For the first time since boyhood he had tears in his eyes.

If he had not been so absorbed by his pain he would have noted that a jay in a nearby tree had flown off, wings flapping silently, and a blackbird in the undergrowth near the hut had departed with its shrill cascading alarm call. As it was, the first noise he became aware of was the crackle of feet on the dry floor of the hut, and his heart sank as he looked round and saw Brock and Ducane looking at him.

"This is Mr. Elliet, my friend," he said. "Suicide. Very sad. I think he was worried about money."

"I see nothing unusual in this hut," Ducane said, and looked at Brock. "Do you?"

"I see nothing," Brock said. "Somebody will find him, I suppose."

"But not us," Ducane said. "Too many complications." He looked at Schorin. "Let's go. Jane and Alice are waiting for lunch."

"If he'd counted the bullets on the table he'd have known there were only five," Schorin said on the way back. "Always keep one up the spout, even when cleaning it, because you never know, that's what they said in Moscow, always keep one up the spout. So Moscow really saved my life. Funny, when you think of it. In fact I believe it is actually a KGB saying."

Ducane and Sugden watched the 'plane carrying Schorin and Alice as it gathered speed and height. Ducane frowned.

"I only hope she'll be happy with him." He sounded worried.

"She'll never be happy *without* him, that's certain," Sugden said.

"Happy ending. So far. I suppose." Ducane sounded doubtful.

"There could be a worse one," Sugden said. He no longer saw the aeroplane, only a shoddy restaurant and a banknote tactfully hidden under a tatty bill.

M42   Ducane looked at him and guessed some of his thoughts.

"You can't win 'em all, Reg," Ducane said softly, and took his arm and turned to lead him to the airport bar.

Recording events in his private diary next day, Brock wrote:

Am relieved that they have finally gone. Jane says that I am a catalyst. I seem to attract troubles and they seek me out. I do nothing to encourage them. She says some people are like that, and it's their misfortune, not their choice, and all they can do is to observe things and try to help where they can. She says catalysts are born, not made, and there is nothing one can do about it. This seems a pity, but she may be right.

Ducane says bugs are all around us, and that Schorin's bedroom in Ebury Street was certainly bugged; not by him but by the KGB. We live in a strange and dangerous period. It is my intention to survive, DV, and I will do anything to do so, or do nothing to do so, as Schorin might say, as circumstances demand. It is the only way a catalyst can act. I trust that all will now be quiet for me in Melford. But I have my doubts, in view of what Jane said.

EPILOGUE

Many months later, and a couple of days after the fishing trip when he had found the mutilated body in a tributary of the Mell, Brock was again writing in his diary. He had just finished when Jane came in with a copy of the Melford evening newspaper. She pointed to a news item on the front page:

JOURNALIST KILLED

Faulty bridge maintainance is believed to have caused the death of a former well known Fleet Street journalist, Mr. Samuel Letts, of Clapham, London, who was staying temporarily in Melford. He was found drowned in a tributary of the Mell.

Recording a verdict of death by misadventure, Dr. Trayer, Acting Coroner, said that Mr. Letts had a head injury which could have been caused if he had leaned against the wall of the Roman bridge, dislodged a big stone, and fallen into the water below, striking his head on a protruding part of the bridge on his way down. Medical evidence and an examination of the bridge, which had a big stone missing, supported this theory.

The coroner added a recommendation that greater attention should be paid to the state of bridges in this country.

Brock put the paper in his briefcase. "I'll have it sent to Alice," he said.

"Won't it upset her, Badge?"

"Anything that removes suspicion from her Alexis Schorin is welcome. We know she was worried about his association with

Sam. The only person who could completely clear Schorin is Schorin—and Schorin rarely tells anybody anything about himself, and when he does it is probably a fairy story."

Brock gave one of his deep sighs. The mind of a Russian always baffled him.